FRACTURED ERA: LEGACY CODE BOOK TWO

PARAGON

AUTUMN KALQUIST

Diapason Publishing

For Juan.
I know it's a long road, and "every month is NaN[o]
but thank you so much for always standing by m[e]
and cheering me on. Your unwavering support a[nd]
love are what keep me going.

CHAPTER ONE

Tadeo's pulse roared in his ears, and the darkness came for him. He'd had this nightmare before. About another girl, in an airlock on a different ship. But this was real. And the airlock control panel in front of him counted down the seconds until it would end.

The traitor, Era Corinth, screamed on the other side of the glass barrier, slamming her fists against it again and again. Red lights flashed in time with the alarms inside the airlock, and their warning drowned out her pleas. The hypnotic pulse of red swept over her tear-stained face, her naked breasts, her bare pregnant stomach.

Bile rose in Tadeo's throat, and he turned his face away. *Kit.* Era reminded him of Kit. Why else would every bone in his body be telling him to save a traitor? Like Era, Kit had been petite, fine-featured, with short hair. And she... Tadeo gritted his teeth and pushed the memories away, like he had so many times before. He stole a glance at Chief Petroff, but the man stood expressionless, hands crossed over his chest.

"Don't do anything stupid, Raines." Chief narrowed his eyes, making the wrinkles around them deepen. "She's a traitor. I meant what I said. I airlocked McGill, and I'll space any other guard who goes in with traitors."

Tadeo focused on the floor, his heart thudding unevenly. Mere minutes ago, he'd nearly freed Era and cost himself his own life. Terrorists on their ship. A traitor in the guard. Era, an innocent-looking girl, tampering with files they needed to settle on a new Earth. Why was all this happening now?

Scuffed tiles, scratched metal, blinking lights. The scene blurred before him.

The thumping of fists against glass stopped.

Tadeo glanced at the airlock, expecting Era to be gone, the airlock wide open, but she stood still. She held one hand to her swollen stomach and gazed down at the infinity tattoo on her other wrist—the symbol of her pairing with the dead husband she'd soon join.

Tadeo's stomach lurched. Era's pregnancy was defective and had been scheduled for termination in a few hours.

"They're lying to all of us about the Defect.... They can save the baby." Era had said that in a final attempt to try to convince them not to airlock her. She was hysterical. Delusional. She'd committed treason, and if he helped her, he'd die with her.

He'd broken the rules once with Kit. He'd never break them again.

The console blinked its final countdown. In ten seconds, Era would be gone, and this nightmare would be over—for her, at least. Sweat dripped down Tadeo's back, and his stiff, navy guard suit stuck to him everywhere, not letting his body heat out or the stale sublevel air in.

00:08
00:07
I can stop it.
00:06
00:05

00:04

00:03

She chose to commit treason. The penalty is death.

00:02

00:01

00:00

Sirens erupted in the control cubic.

Era was gone.

Tadeo's chest tightened. The dark void of space gaped at him from the empty airlock, and he glimpsed the planet the fleet orbited—a half-circle of deep red. *Soren.* Swirling clouds the color of rust moved across its surface, and down below, noxious air and dust choked life from anyone suicidal enough to walk its surface.

Suicide. Era was gone, like she'd never existed. They'd never retrieve her body, and they'd rule this a suicide. Which is exactly what the president wanted.

Chief gestured to Era's discarded suit and boots, and Tadeo grabbed them and followed him into the corridor.

The door slid shut behind them, and the heat and deep hum of the power core replaced the blaring sirens. Long, thin lume bars

PARAGON

flickered from the ceiling every few feet, unevenly illuminating the scarred metal walls.

As Tadeo followed the chief down the corridor, his mind raced, trying to grapple with what had just happened. They passed a long row of storage cubics, finally coming to the one Nyssa had interrogated Era in.

The chief swiped his shift card across the scanner, and the cubic opened, revealing a small room with a single metal chair and silver case. The chief grabbed the case and shut the door. The lume bar above them flickered in an uneven rhythm, highlighting Chief's silver-brown hair and bringing out the harsh lines on his face.

"Lieutenant Raines."

Tadeo stood straighter, throwing his shoulders back at the tone in Chief's voice. Guard training had ingrained it in him, made it a habit.

"Yes, sir." Tadeo's voice came out deep and strong, like he wasn't ready to puke all over the chipped, grease-coated tiles.

"Night shift bridge crew will see the alarm on their consoles soon," Chief said roughly. "They'll send an emergency maintenance crew down the main stairwell to close the airlock.

I'm taking stairwell B to the president. Take C. Shred the husband's shift card on command level and drop the traitor's clothes down the textile recyc chute. Understood?"

Tadeo tightened his grip on Era's suit and boots, and a hand went to his pocket, tracing the shape of her husband's shift card.

"Raines. Do you understand?"

Tadeo focused on Chief's creased face. The president had said this all had to be done in secret—that the colonists would panic if they found out Era had tampered with the archives.

But who else had they interrogated down here—airlocked without anyone knowing? McGill had been Chief's right-hand man before he'd been sent away—no, before Chief had *airlocked* him.

"Yes... sir. But Chief—about McGill..."

Chief's nostrils flared, and he stepped closer, poking a finger at Tadeo's chest. "You keep your mouth shut about him. No one needs to know we had a traitor in the guard. Not anyone. That's classified information."

"But, sir, how..." Tadeo's voice came out strained, uncomprehending. "He was in the president's guard—he was second only to you."

"And now, by the *president's* choice, it appears *you* have replaced him—"

"But how did you—"

"McGill was a traitor," Chief sneered. "You don't need to know the specifics. Lieutenant Raines, do *you* sympathize with the traitors? Because that's what it looked like back there."

Tadeo clenched his jaw tight. "No, sir."

"Then do not misstep again. Do not ever disobey a direct order. I wouldn't want to airlock the heir to the *Meso*, but I'm sure they'd have no problem finding your replacement."

Tadeo swallowed back the bitter taste in his mouth and challenged the chief's hostile glare with one of his own. That this man, a former tech, should be the president's most trusted guard, and Tadeo, son of a captain, had to do everything he said without question... it wasn't right. But the chief had earned his position, and Tadeo would do his duty for as long as he was in the guard.

"Answer me, Raines. Do you understand?"

"Yes. Yes, sir."

"You do not speak of this mission. Not to anyone."

"I understand, sir."

"Recyc those things," he said, pointing to Era's belongings, "then meet me at command level lounge. The president wants to brief you. Don't get caught."

He turned and strode down the corridor, silver metal case in his grasp, and didn't look back.

Tadeo wiped the sweat from his brow and started running. A rush of adrenaline surged through his veins as he headed down a side corridor. He sprinted past dented metal walls and turned left at the first cross-corridor, toward stairwell C. The main stairwell met this sector, and if he didn't get through it fast enough, the emergency crew might see him.

Most of the fleet's recent traitors had been subs, working down here. Miles of dark corridors, hidden spaces to do things you didn't want to be caught doing. The sublevels were the seedy underbelly of every ship—the place where you could get away with breaking the rules. Kit resurfaced in his mind, along with the thrill he'd felt every time he'd broken the rules with her. This felt like that. Exciting. *Forbidden.*

The corridor widened, and high ceilings replaced the cramped feel of the earlier sectors. The hum of the power core was even louder here, and the acrid scent of hot metal reached his nostrils. He slowed to a walk to get his bearings.

Tangles of thick metal pipes extended deep into the sector on either side of him, and a low barrier comprised of metal slats separated the walkway from the pipes. Was this sector heating—or life support? He was certain this was the way to stairwell C, but he didn't know the sublevel sectors well on this ship.

Loud voices echoed down the corridor and seemed to bounce off the ceiling and meld with the vibrations of the core. Another shot of adrenaline spiked through Tadeo, and his heart beat a wild rhythm against his rib cage. He could *not* be seen down here.

He glanced around, but there was nowhere to hide unless he leapt over the barrier. The space between the metal slats and the pipes left barely enough room to stand, and he didn't have protective gear on. *Let's hope they aren't heating.*

He leaned over the barrier closest to him and spit. His saliva hit the nearest pipe and oozed down the rusted metal. Not heating, then.

The voices grew louder. Tadeo dropped Era's belongings over the divide and took one more look down the empty corridor. Then he leapt over the barrier sideways, wedging his body in the tight space.

Every muscle tensed as he peered out between the slats, and sweat burned his eyes. Would they come this way? Would they see him? His navy blue guard uniform might blend in with the dirty gray color of the pipes behind him. Maybe.

He should be afraid, worried, but all he felt was a thrill at the thought of getting caught. Then he saw it.

Kak.

His shift card lay on the floor, bright white against the grease-stained tiles. His throat constricted, and the thrill faded. His card must have been knocked off his suit when he dove over the barrier. If the subs saw it and picked it up, they'd know he was down here when Era died.

"The maintenance airlock," one of them called.

They were close. Too close for him to get to the card in time.

"Sector seven," yelled another.

PARAGON

Tadeo held his breath and counted the sets of boots as they pounded past. Four sets. The sublevel emergency crew.

Not a single boot touched his card.

When their voices receded, he let out a breath, waited several more seconds, then hauled himself over the divide. He grabbed Era's gear, shoved his card in his pocket, and took off down the corridor.

His chest lightened, and a giddy feeling overtook him, the old feeling of doing something wrong and getting away with it.

He sprinted faster, pushing himself, and his muscles responded, remembering what it was like when he had free run of the *Meso*. How he'd run the open levels of the deka he grew up on for miles and miles.

He didn't slow down until he reached stairwell C.

Tadeo bounded up the stairs, the only sound his own boots echoing through the shaft. No one should be moving through here at this hour, not during night shift—since the president had instituted a mandatory curfew.

As he rounded each landing, his gaze hit the numbers engraved in the metal doors. When he reached level seven, command level, his legs ached from his rapid ascent. He rested his hands on his knees and took deep breaths. There would normally be guards standing here, but not tonight. Chief had made sure of that. He almost smiled at his success.

I just airlocked a girl.

A sick feeling raced through him, killing his buzz. He wiped his brow and unzipped his pocket to draw out his shift card.

When he passed it over the scanner, a red light came on. The scanner beeped a warning.

Bloody piece of kak. He ran the card again. Another beep, and the red light blinked, insistent he didn't have the clearance to access this level.

Tadeo stiffened and slowly looked down at the card in his hand. It was scuffed, dirt and grease embedded in the scratched surface. It was far too filthy for the brief moment it had been on the sublevel floor. Tadeo turned it over, and his heart rate sped up again as he saw the name stamped on the card.

DRITAN CORINTH.

Era's *husband's* shift card. He fought the urge to drop the thing. Dritan had died on mining duty on Soren, but before that, he'd worked in the sublevels. They'd used

PARAGON

his card to access the airlock, so it would look like Era had taken advantage of her husband's access to kill herself.

Now it would be logged into the system *after* Era had supposedly used it to commit suicide out a maintenance airlock. He'd fucked up. Majorly.

Tadeo shoved the card back in his pocket and clutched Era's boots and suit closer, hands trembling as he patted his other pockets for his own card. He briefly considered going back down a level and taking a different route.

If anyone checked the records...

But they wouldn't. No one would check. They had no reason to. Chief gave the orders, and he knew what really happened. There'd be no real investigation. And if there was, Chief would take care of it. Everyone would believe Era went out the airlock with that card.

He found his own and took a deep breath as he passed it over the scanner. This time the light turned green.

CHAPTER TWO

Fresh air filled Tadeo's lungs as he entered command level. The lume bars gleamed at quarter-power, as they had in the stairwell, but they all worked, unlike in the sublevels. The tiles were scuffed, but still white and uncracked. Everything was newer, cleaner up here—here where he really belonged. Tadeo's boots squeaked against the tiles; the only other sound was the life support fans whirring in the night.

Dritan's card seemed to heat up and give off a glow in his pocket. If anyone chose that moment to open their cubic, make their way to the shared lavs... they'd wonder what he was doing, in full guard uniform, carrying a tech suit and boots in the dead of night shift. He needed to do this fast, get it over with, and go meet Chief and the president.

He hurried through the level, listening for the whoosh of doors opening in the corridors, but soon he was past living quarters, and he reached recyc at the back of the level.

Chutes lined the far wall, each labeled with the type of recyc they accommodated. Tadeo breathed hard as he tossed Era's boots down the textile chute and then opened all the pockets on her suit, checking for her shift card or anything else that could identify the ex-owner. But her pockets were empty. He tossed the suit down after the boots.

A series of shredders and compactors stood against the opposite wall, and Tadeo worked fast, shredding Dritan's card in the machine designed to break down plastic. As the tiny flecks dropped into the bin, his shoulders relaxed, the tight knot in his gut dissipated. He sent the chips down the plastic recyc chute.

As the last of the evidence disappeared, the dregs of Tadeo's adrenaline drained from his system and left his legs wobbly.

He grunted, sinking against the wall to support himself, and stared blankly at the recyc chutes.

Era's wide brown eyes leaking tears, one palm over her swollen stomach, that damn infinity tattoo on her wrist.

He glanced down at his own wrist, at the teardrop shape there—one-half of an infinity symbol. He'd get the whole thing—like Era's—when he paired.

Zephyr. What would he tell her? He'd been spending time with her lately... acting like they were matching up. She'd seemed close to Era. But Zephyr was the future captain of the *London*. There was no way she could have known what Era was really into.

I killed her.

His hands shook as he ran them through his hair, pushing the long dark strands out of his face. A heavy weight grew in his chest and made it hard to breathe. He'd helped airlock colonists before. But never like this, in secret. And never a pregnant girl, though the pregnancy had been defective anyway. Why did she have to commit treason? Why did she force them to airlock her?

Tadeo tried to banish her from his mind. He'd followed the laws, done what was necessary. If he couldn't handle this, how would he ever lead his own ship?

Willing his legs to strengthen, he pushed away from the wall. What he wouldn't give for just a little grimp right now. It'd kill his roiling emotions, deaden his senses. But he'd get addicted again, and nothing was worth that.

The corridors were silent, eerie in the low light as he made his way to the command level lounge.

Chief Petroff was waiting for him there—a silent, heavy shadow in the dim light. He glanced up and down the empty corridor, then focused on Tadeo. "What took so long? Did you run into any problems?"

Tadeo straightened his shoulders under the scrutiny. He'd accidentally used Dritan's shift card, but Chief didn't need to know that. "Emergency crew passed me by, but I wasn't seen, sir."

"Good. Everything went down the chutes?"

"Yes, sir."

The chief led Tadeo down several corridors, and despite the dim light, everything gleamed brighter the further they went. They were heading to the executive living quarters, where the president, board, and crew families lived. Tadeo lived on command level, but his quarters weren't this new or this big. He hadn't been in this sector in years, not since he and his mother had visited the president. The doors got further apart as the quarters grew in size, until they reached double doors at the end of the final corridor.

When Chief knocked, the doors opened immediately, and Nyssa Sorenson stepped into the frame. She'd taken off the suit she'd worn earlier and had exchanged it for a loose-fitting, white leisure jumpsuit. Her blond hair was usually tied back in a severe bun, but now it hung in waves around her lined face, softening it, making her look far younger than her forty-five years. And making Tadeo feel like the child he'd been the last time he was here.

But when her pale blue eyes met his, suddenly Tadeo could think of only one word to describe her.

Ruthless.

She'd been the one to order Era's death. *And McGill's.* She did what needed to be done. Before tonight, he'd been a loyal member of the president's guard, the favored son of a deka captain, only addressing Nyssa in passing. But now? The entire dynamic between them had changed. What they'd all done seemed to weigh heavily in the charged silence—as if the recycled air would be poisoned by deeds better left unspoken.

"Chief, wait outside," Nyssa finally said, her voice low. "Come in, Lieutenant Raines."

Tadeo stole an uneasy glance at Petroff, and the chief narrowed his eyes at Tadeo, displeased. But he crossed his arms in front of him and leaned against the wall to wait.

Tadeo stepped into the president's quarters, and the doors slid closed behind them. Nyssa walked away, toward her galley nook, and got out metal glasses and a bottle of quin liquor.

As she poured the liquid, Tadeo glanced around. Her quarters were like the captain's quarters aboard the *Meso*, only larger. Like *home*. Despite the tension, his muscles relaxed involuntarily. The space gleamed with new metal panels on every wall. It was decorated with plush couches and well-lit by bright lume bars. A strip of glasstex ran the length of the far wall, revealing dark space beyond, and Tadeo knew that if you turned out all the lights, sometimes you could see the other ships in the fleet.

There were ten ships out there, all smaller than the flagship *Paragon*, but all identical—vast cities of glinting metal. Inside each deka, the machinery and colonists worked hard to produce supplies for the fleet. Especially for the *Paragon*, which carried the greatest number of colonists.

But it was the stars he'd stared at most as they'd journeyed. Any one of them might nurture life on a new Earth they hadn't yet discovered.

Would anyone look out a strip of glasstex this shift and see Era's body? His stomach turned, and he ripped his eyes from the glass. He took a deep breath as Nyssa carried the drinks over, and he inhaled the clean, soothing scent of the room. Several hydropods were pushed up against the walls, their greens filling the air with the sweet smell of life, mingling with the lavender scent of executive standard soap.

Nyssa handed him a cup and sat down on one of the deep blue couches. "You may sit," she said, gesturing to the couch on the other side of a low, metal table.

Tadeo walked to the couch and sank into the soft upholstery.

Nyssa leaned back on the other couch and took a sip of her drink. "Everything went smoothly, I trust?"

His suit felt as though it tightened around every pore in his body, suffocating him. Everything *had* gone smoothly, except when he'd used Dritan's shift card. He should tell her, but... "Yes. We followed your orders."

"Good," she said, her expression veiled. "No one must know the girl tampered with the archives—or anything about what happened tonight."

"I understand... Madame President." Tadeo took a sip of his drink, feeling awkward. The liquid burned a trail down his throat.

"We can drop the formalities in here, Tadeo. Call me Nyssa."

Tadeo nodded, unable to speak.

"Did the traitor say anything else to you tonight?"

He furrowed his brow. He didn't want to think of this, relive it again already. He swallowed more of his drink, and a fire lit up in his stomach. "What do you mean?"

The president lifted a brow. "Did she say anything that sounded like treason to you? Anything suspicious?"

"No. She... She denied she committed a crime."

"Anything else?"

"She was hysterical. She started saying..." Tadeo's throat thickened. Whatever the traitor said was irrelevant, wasn't it? "She said the Defect was a lie."

"She would have said anything to save herself." Nyssa leaned forward, and her blue eyes locked onto his. "It had to be done this way. She erased files we needed to settle on a new Earth. That's a crime that cannot be forgiven."

Tadeo slowly nodded. "I understand."

Era deserved her punishment. Nyssa made the hard choices when they needed to be made, which was what good leaders did—what his mother did. Which was what *he* would do as a leader.

"I've always trusted you and your mother. But you truly proved your loyalty tonight." Nyssa stood and walked over to the glasstex, cup in hand. She gazed out at the depths of space. "These are hard times. We don't know who we can trust."

Tadeo grunted a reply and took another sip, wishing this clandestine meeting were over.

After a moment, she turned to face him. "I believe Era may have been working with other traitors."

Tadeo's pulse quickened, and he sat up straight. "More traitors on the *Paragon*?"

"Yes. Era confessed knowledge that others work against us. But she didn't have names."

Tadeo set his cup down on the table. "You think traitors could be planning more attacks here... like the hull breach?" *Or like the attack on Tesmee?* He didn't say it but glanced toward the doors at the far end of the room. Tesmee would be asleep in one of those cubics.

Nyssa shook her head. "We were unable to get that information. But Era's husband did work down in the sublevels with the terrorists. Perhaps he recruited Era to his cause."

"But... wasn't Dritan Corinth the one who *named* the terrorists—the one who turned them in? I thought he was absolved."

"Yes. But perhaps we were wrong about him."

"What about the rest of his crew—and the crews we sent to Soren?"

Nyssa took a deep breath and slowly traced the infinity symbol engraved on the glass with one finger. It matched the one on her wrist perfectly. "We investigated every person the terrorists worked with. And every one of them is dead. I *thought* the problem had been taken care of. Clearly it has not. We arrested some other sublevel workers for speaking treason, but they haven't given us any leads. They'll be heading down to Soren before first shift on the transport."

Since they'd airlocked the traitors, they'd gotten more reports of colonists speaking treason. The brig was filling up with offenders. Pretty soon, they'd run out of space. The president was smart. Sending them to Soren would shut them up and serve as a warning to the rest.

"We need to continue our search for traitors," Nyssa said, her voice strong. She walked back over to the couch and sat down. "We must solve this problem. Permanently."

Tadeo's heart rate quickened, and he leaned toward her. "Tell me what I need to do."

Nyssa's mouth turned up a little. "I'm lucky to have you in my guard, Tadeo. I knew I could trust you to take care of this. I believe Era may have stolen data from the archives and hidden it somewhere for the other traitors to find. And if she did, I need you to find it before her co-conspirators do."

Tadeo worked his jaw. "If she did, I'll find it. But... what exactly am I looking for?"

"A cube, I think, maybe more than one cube. Chief has her records. You will have access to *anything* you need." Nyssa pursed her lips. "Choose another guard you trust, and search every sector Era frequented. Begin on first shift, and try not to draw attention to yourself. Search her cubic first. If you don't find anything, search every inch of the Repository. Then move on to any other places Era visited in the past few weeks."

"And what about the head archivist? Is she under suspicion?"

"Not at this time, no. But we'll be watching her."

"What should I tell her?"

"You just tell her and everyone else that it's a confidential investigation regarding Era's suicide."

A whoosh sounded from the far wall, and Tadeo turned, rigid. Tesmee stepped out of a darkened cubic wearing a loose-fitting, white leisure suit like Nyssa's. Her earth-Asian features were nothing like Nyssa's—she looked just like her father. She lifted a thin wrist to shield her eyes from the bright light of the lume bars.

"Mother? Who are you talking... to?" Her

dark eyes widened as noticed Tadeo, and she smoothed back her sleep-tousled hair.

"Tesmee," Nyssa said. "Get back in your cubic. Now."

Tesmee waved at Tadeo, obviously trying to show off the tear-shaped tattoo on her wrist, like usual. It was as if she wanted to remind him she was a fourteen-year-old half now and not the child of ten she'd been when he'd first arrived.

"Lieutenant Raines. I didn't know you were stopping by." She glanced up at the lume bars, still at half-light, clearly confused. "Wait. What shift is it?"

"Get back in your cubic." Nyssa stood up. "I'll be in to talk with you in a minute."

Tesmee looked like she wanted to argue, but she crossed her arms and pouted instead, looking like a kid in caretaker sector. Nyssa stared her down, and Tesmee finally relented, turning heel and heading back into her cubic. The door slid shut behind her.

Ever since Tesmee's father had died in a mysterious transport accident, Nyssa never really let her off command level. And since a terrorist had just tried to kill Tesmee, her confinement had only grown more restrictive. No wonder she didn't know what shift it was. Tadeo would go insane if someone kept him locked away like that.

Nyssa came around to him and rested a hand on his sleeve. "I promised your mother I'd allow you to contact her on the private bridge comm. You have my permission to access it. Once all of this is over."

"I—"

"We have much to discuss, but now is not the time." She guided him back to the door and opened it.

Chief stood in the corridor, arms still crossed. "It's all clear," he said.

"The second you find anything like what I described," Nyssa said to Tadeo, "bring it straight to me or Chief Petroff."

"I will, Madame President."

CHAPTER THREE

Air.

Dritan sucked in a breath and coughed. He lurched to the side, and pain shot through him. His right arm didn't work like it should, didn't feel normal. He fumbled in his suit for an emergency glow bar and pulled it out, shaking it until it illuminated his surroundings.

Rock, all around. A bloodied arm, crushed and disembodied under a large boulder next to him. Another, up ahead, in the shadows. More blood, closer. Guts trailing from a dead man.

Dritan's empty stomach heaved, and he collapsed against a jagged rock wall, the scene blurring before him. *What was I looking for?*

He glanced down. His mask lay beside him, crumpled—*empty*—oxygen packs next to it. He'd used up all his oxygen. Spots of light drifted across the packs, and he shook his head.

You need air, Dritan. Find air.

"Era?" Dritan sat up straighter. A weight settled in him, a terrible sense that he couldn't save them both from this.

No. He was on Soren. Era was safe. Up on the *Paragon*.

And he was suffocating.

He tucked his mask and canteen into his work belt and staggered toward the figure to his right. Blinding pain coursed through his injured arm, and he cried out. He stopped, panting.

The air's bad, he heard Era say.

Dritan shook his head and ground his teeth against the pain as he dragged himself over the sharp rocks. He was hallucinating as the poisonous air stole his life away. He had to find an oxygen pack. But there was barely enough room to crawl, and the rock walls seemed to grow closer as he moved.

He raised his glow bar, casting a faint blue light over his imme- diate area. Two of his crew mates lay beneath an enormous rock, thick, viscous blood pooled beneath them, their limbs splayed at awkward angles. Pricks of light danced across Dritan's vision as he edged around the bodies.

Oxygen, his Era hallucination insisted again.

"Oxygen." His heart thudded against his chest, and he gasped, trying to suck in air. He moved closer to the crushed bodies and searched the twisted limbs for signs of a work belt. There. One still had a few oxygen packs and a helio.

As he pulled the packs and helio from the belt, his trembling fingertips touched a cold white length of bone jutting from the man's torso. He shuddered, and his world slid toward the black nothing of space.

Air.

The darkness wasn't his glow bar dying. *He was dying.* He blinked against the black and rushed to twist a new oxygen pack onto his mask. He inhaled. Once, twice, three times he breathed in the metallic taste of the liquid-packed oxygen. Soon the spots of light dancing across his mangled crew faded. He tried to survey the scene, but his glow bar barely lit two feet in front of him. He picked up the helio. *Please work.*

He tapped the cool, metal sphere, and it floated into the air and brightened, its yellow glow warmer than the cool sun Soren orbited. The helio illuminated a wider space, allowing him to make his way around the fallen debris. Was he the only one left? Memories tried to surface in Dritan's mind, but everything was foggy, disjointed.

Then he caught sight of another body, half buried in scree. A woman, her bloodied white-blond hair matted to her head. *Janet Lanar.* A fellow sub from the old *Paragon* crew. She had a mask on, but her oxygen pack was flat, nearly empty. Was it a trick of the light, or was her chest still moving? He made his way to her, wincing against the pain in his arm, and crouched before her.

"Jan." He replaced her oxygen pack with unsteady hands. "Jan, can you hear me?"

Her eyelids fluttered, and he let out a breath. He used his good arm to pull the lightweight rocks off her body, then shook her again. This time, she let out a moan.

Two survivors. Dritan sat back on his heels and took a few more breaths. His mind began to clear as he struggled to make sense of it all, fought to remember how long they'd been trapped down here. He inhaled again, taking less oxygen this time.

Jan finally opened her eyes, and Dritan offered her his good arm to help her sit up. "You okay?"

"Yeah, I... I don't think anything's broken," Jan said, her voice muffled by the mask. "Is anyone else...?"

Dritan shook his head, and Jan's face darkened.

"I thought I was done for in that last quake," she said. "How'd you survive? I guess those guys you knew from the *London* were right. You got some kinda lucky gene."

Lucky.

Dritan lifted his canteen from his belt and shook it. There was a little water left. He unscrewed the lid with one shaking hand and gave it to Jan. She lifted her mask to sip it, and he did the same.

"I don't remember..." he said.

Then everything came rushing back—each moment outlined in his mind as surely being his last.

They were expanding the subcity on Soren, just like Era had thought, and he'd been ordered to help clear tunnels for a new sector. Forty men and women—five full crews—loaded into rockcrawlers and were dropped off over a mile outside the main subcity.

They placed a charge near the end of the massive cavern. It should have blown a small hole in the rock, but instead... something went very wrong. The explosion was bigger than they planned. There were screams, so many screams. Dritan fell beneath the rubble, dazed, sounds of the dying echoing off the high ceiling. Then the cavern collapsed, trapping them all.

But there were a few survivors, and they worked together to find the way to the exit that led back up to the poisonous surface. Then, one of the many quakes that plagued the planet had brought down even more rock.

He reached a hand to his head, and blood came away on his fingertips. A small gash. He was injured, but alive at least. The others...

"It's definitely been more than forty-eight hours," Jan said.

Dritan nodded and helped her to her feet. "The rescue crews might think we're all dead, but someone's gonna come eventually. We just need to focus on finding more oxygen and water—so we can survive until they do."

Jan leaned on him, and they helped each other step around the fallen rocks as they assessed their situation.

"We were working over there—they thought the exit was that direction." Dritan pointed toward a series of dark crevices.

"Are you sure?"

"Yes."

Dritan cradled his bad arm and scanned the area, trying not to look too hard at his fallen crewmates. He didn't want to know who they were. Who they *had been*. "We need to search all the bodies. Move the rocks to find supplies."

"Corinth?" Jan lightly touched his arm.

"What?"

"I didn't want to say it when the others were still..."

Dritan waited, but she didn't finish. "Just say it."

"That explosion wasn't right."

Dritan looked down at Jan. "We followed procedure. Something went wrong—the cavern was unstable."

"No," Jan's deep blue eyes met his. "I originally came from mining—from the *Perth*."

"I didn't know that."

"My parents managed to get me off there—and now here I am... buried beneath rock anyway." Jan knit her brows together. "As a half, I helped mine the meteors a few times."

"And...?"

"And I saw the charge the guys planted down here. It didn't have enough powder to cause that kind of explosion. Nowhere near enough. The Artex powder had to be augmented. With... Zenith or something, as crazy as that sounds."

A bitter taste rose in Dritan's mouth, and he risked another small sip of their water. "I don't understand. Zenith?"

"It increases the power of a blast. But, my point is... What if no rescue's coming?" Jan said. "What if... what if this wasn't an accident? All the crews from *Paragon* were on this mission."

Dritan shook his head. "No. No way. We had nothing to do with—"

"With the *terrorists*?" Her eyes narrowed. "But we did. We worked alongside them. And that was treason enough. That's why they sent us all here—to get rid of us."

"No," Dritan said firmly. He walked away from her, toward the cluster of boulders, more bodies crushed beneath them. "They sent us because everyone has to serve a term here. We all need to do our part."

"They sent us here to send everyone a *message*," Jan said, her voice rising. "How many others in the fleet would be happy to see the president—the board—dead? My family's up there on the *Paragon*. I need to protect them. And I'm... stuck here. What if it's not safe up there either?"

Dritan's gut twisted. Era. *I have to get back to Era. And to our baby.* But he didn't say it. He hunkered down beside the bodies and reached his hand beneath the boulder, eyes closed, feeling around until his hand touched a work belt. One more oxygen pack. He pulled it out slowly, fighting the urge to vomit as the corpse squished against his arm. He stood up and took a step back, staring down at the pack. "The *Paragon* is safe now."

"How do you know?" Jan's voice cracked, and her eyes went a little wild. "And what if there are colonists like Sam, Tati, and Jonas still up there? They talked to so many others—

not just us. All those people are still up there on the *Paragon*. Did you know Tati even had a lover? My husband Gavin told me the rumor. But no one seemed to know who it was. What if—"

"Stop it. Our families are safe up there," Dritan repeated. He went to Jan and squeezed her arm until her fearful gaze met his. "We need to focus on surviving. Rescue will come. They won't leave us here."

Jan let out a harsh laugh and grimaced against some pain inside her. She pulled her arm away and leaned against a rock. "If they think sending us down here will stop people from talking treason—they're wrong. All of us dying down here—it'll be like dumping Artex on a fire."

"We're *not* going to die. And don't say that kak."

"Who's going to hear me? Is it fair all the subs have to die young to take care of the rest of the fleet? When's the last time they sent a crew of techs to blow a hole in rock?"

"Is it fair? I don't know. But it's not their job. It's ours. We all have to play our part so this fleet—"

"Corinth. Are you listening to yourself?"

Jan focused on Dritan's face, clearly trying not to look at the corpses behind him. "I'm worried about my family. Aren't you?"

Dritan pulled at his short curls, thinking of Era—alone on the *Paragon*—and winced as his fingers brushed the gash on his head. "Look. Others might talk, but that's all they do. Talk. The terrorists did more than just talk. They crossed a line. And they're dead now. People will see that—no one else will want to cross that line."

"I wish they'd succeeded," Jan said through gritted teeth. "I shouldn't *be* here. *We* wouldn't be here if they had."

Heat spread in Dritan's chest. "Succeeded in what? Blowing a hole in exec sector?" He stepped toward her. "Killing the president and the board? Everyone has a place in the fleet. That is theirs. This is ours. It's how we *all* survive."

"What if getting rid of them *is* the only way to survive? What if... doing the right thing means doing the wrong thing?" Jan's eyes went to the bodies beneath the rocks, and her jaw went tight.

Dritan closed his eyes, and the anger drained from him. Tati, Jonas, and Sam had all talked treason. And when Dritan saw Sam attack the president's daughter—when he'd realized the three of them caused the hull breach, he'd turned on them—turned on his own people. Subs never turned on each other. Shame flooded him, but he pushed it down. *I did the right thing.*

"Yeah," he said, "sometimes doing the right thing means doing the wrong thing. But I draw the line at trying to take someone else's life."

Jan licked her lips. "They take ours. And maybe this accident wasn't an accident. Maybe no one is coming for us."

Dritan swallowed and met her gaze. She was wrong. He was loyal, and he'd proved it to the president. No one had a reason to want them dead. "We need to focus on the here and *now*. On surviving. Get it together, Lanar. The *Paragon*'s safe, and there's no conspiracy to kill us."

Jan pressed her lips together, and her eyes shone in the yellow light of the helio. "I just want to see my daughter again."

"And you will. We will *both* see our families." He slid the oxygen pack into his work belt and turned away from her.

PARAGON

He was *not* going to die down here. He'd been a small child when his parents went to fix a hull breach and never came back. And he wouldn't leave Era and their baby the way his parents had left him. He was getting off this damn planet.

He started around the boulders, searching for more of his fallen crewmates. He'd made it three feet when another quake reverberated beneath his boots. His heart sped up, and he snatched the helio from the air, crouching low against a boulder as more rocks began to fall. He closed his eyes and pictured Era as the planet shook around him.

The day they paired. Her laughing brown eyes. The feel of her lips against his, holding her in his arms. Would he ever see her again?

She had been laughing on their way to the tattoo cubic. She even smiled through the pain of the infinity tattoo, so proud to finally leave her half status behind. Afterward, they had a special meal up on command level. Something Zephyr smuggled out of the galley for them.

"I never thought I'd feel this happy again," Era said, her bright eyes meeting his over a meal better than any Dritan had ever eaten.

"Now you'll have to live in paired couples sector with me," he replied. "You won't get to live up here on command level anymore."

"I don't care. I've told you—I'll be happy anywhere, as long as I'm with *you*."

Era needed him, like no one else ever had. He *had* to get back to her.

The quake seemed to last forever, but finally, it ended. Dritan stood, his legs weak as fresh poured metal. His "lucky gene" had saved him again.

"Dritan," Jan called, her voice weak.

He released the helio, and it floated beside him as he pushed around the new debris, seeking her.

"Jan!" Dust flew through the air, obscuring his vision.

"I'm here."

Dritan moved through the dust and found her. She was trapped against the rock wall, a trail of red running down her head and neck. An enormous boulder pinned her leg to the ground, and blood gushed from it, pooling beneath her. She turned her head, pale eyes watering, and a whimper croaked from her throat.

PARAGON

He reached her just as her eyes fluttered shut.

CHAPTER FOUR

Blackness enveloped Tadeo, and he sensed he'd stayed in his bunk too long. But when he lay here in the dark, he could pretend Kit was still alive—that he was still on the *Meso*, and he could run down to the sublevels and meet her there. In secret. Breaking the rules.

I killed them. Era... and Kit.

He hadn't felt this bad since he first got to the *Paragon*. Grimp would make it all go away. But his mother had made sure no one on medlevel would give it to him. She'd saved him from his addiction and his grief.

Tadeo opened his eyes, blinking in the darkness to banish the vision of pregnant Era—standing naked in the airlock, staring down at the infinity symbol on her wrist, tears streaming down her face. *This* nightmare would not follow him around every waking shift, because Era had deserved to die.

He sat up and slammed a hand against the switch beside his bunk. The lume bars in his sleeping compartment flickered to life, and Tadeo groaned, tossing his sweat-soaked blanket to the floor. He rose, naked, and walked across his cubic.

His muscles ached from his run through the sublevels the night before, but the spongy rubber tiles felt cool under his feet, and the drafty air chilled his overheated skin. The small, square holo screen on his wall displayed the time. *Kak.* He was late for mess again.

When he reached his lav unit, he turned on the faucet and splashed water on his face. He glanced at himself in the cracked mirror. A hunk of his black hair hung in his bloodshot brown eyes. He pushed it off his forehead and smoothed it back. "You're an idiot."

Why couldn't he forget Kit? He gripped the edges of the sink and tried to focus. There were traitors on this ship. And today he needed to find whatever it was Era had stolen for them.

PARAGON

Tadeo's comcuff went off from inside the curved metal cabinet bolted to the wall. He pulled it out and checked the ID. It was Darren Omar, son of the *Vancouver*'s navigator, and one of Tadeo's few true peers on this ship. He was the closest thing Tadeo had ever had to a friend here. Tadeo sighed and pressed the button to answer it.

"Raines."

"Where are you?"

"My bunk."

"Seriously? I figured. You're late for mess. Again."

"I'll get there."

"Yeah, you will."

A loud bang resonated from Tadeo's door. He groaned and walked over to open it, realizing at the last second he was still naked.

"Kak, man." Omar's eyes widened, bright against his black skin, and he shielded them with one hand. "I don't go like that."

Tadeo's gut twisted at the remark, but he smirked at Omar with forced amusement. He knew what some people said about him—that he didn't like women—just because he hadn't paired with anyone yet. But people also whispered he'd seduced a girl back on the *Meso*—

and then she'd disappeared. He'd rather them believe he didn't like women than the rumors that came so close to the truth.

Tadeo stepped out of the way, spreading his arm wide. "Come on in."

Omar pressed his lips together, clearly embarrassed by what he'd insinuated. He focused on Tadeo's face, trying not to look at the rest of him, and reluctantly crossed the threshold, keeping his distance.

Tadeo took his time walking back to his cabinet, forcing Omar to feel discomfort at his full-on nudity. He pulled a fresh guard suit out, and as he stepped into it, he gestured to the small couch across from his bunk. "You can sit."

Omar ran a hand over his shaved head and sank down on the bench, averting his eyes as Tadeo suited up. Once he zipped his suit, Omar's shoulders relaxed, and he leaned back against the wall panel.

"Wow," Omar said, glancing around at Tadeo's spacious quarters. "You have your own lav? Damn. My new cubic's half this size. When do I get one of these?"

"Never. Just be happy you're not *sharing* with bunkmates any- more."

Tadeo had lived in the guard barracks for four years—until his promotion to the president's guard. When Tadeo moved up, he'd pulled for Omar to get promoted, too. But Tadeo had gotten a better cubic because he was the heir to the *Meso*. And Omar... wasn't.

"Hurry up man, we're gonna miss mess."

"You know, you don't have to caretake me," Tadeo said in a mocking tone. "Unless you feel like getting demoted to caretaker sector. You wanna guard the kids?"

"Do *you* wanna guard kids?" Omar fired right back. "'Cause Chief wasn't too happy with you earlier. You need to learn to answer your comm. He tried to comm you before mess, but you didn't answer. So he commed me, and since he just *happened* to have me on the cuff, he ordered me to run those treason talkers down to the hangar bay. How 'bout you answer your damn cuff next time, yeah?"

Tadeo attached his comcuff to his wrist, slipped in his earbud, and holstered his pulse gun to his belt. Omar was one of the few guards who didn't act like he was going to piss himself whenever Tadeo talked to him. He liked that about him. That, and he didn't ask too many questions, despite the rumors about Tadeo.

"Are the treason talkers going somewhere?" Tadeo asked, feigning surprise.

"The president and board decided to send 'em down to Soren."

"They finished questioning them?"

"Yeah," Omar said. "They weren't happy. They talked kak about the president and board. Said they fight all the time, and that's the reason the jumpgate's not done. Doesn't matter what they think now, though. They're on their way to Soren."

Tadeo tightened his jaw. The board sometimes did stand in the way of progress, but the fleet had to follow the laws it had made for itself, or everything would disintegrate long before they reached New Earth.

"Tough kak for them," Tadeo said. "Let's get to mess."

Omar and Tadeo headed toward command level galley, and two girls walked by, daughters of some bridge crew member or another. He should remember their names after four years on this ship, but he didn't. They stared at him as they walked past, one whispering something to the other. Omar smiled broadly at them, but they didn't pay attention to him, because their eyes were glued to Tadeo. Omar let out an exaggerated sigh at their disinterest, but Tadeo just frowned and kept his eyes straight ahead.

They entered the galley, and the scents from the buffet wafted over them. Tadeo's stomach growled in response. It was a small room, tiny compared to the guard galley or the massive main galley. A few tall, white hydropods stood at the corners of the room, and leaves hung over the edges of each ovoid pod. Rare greenery on the flagship. He suppressed a pang of homesickness. The president and command galley might have plants, but the *Paragon* was seriously short on green. Some considered this to be the best ship in the fleet, but it would never be that to him.

Farida Mittal, the youngest member of the board, sat next to Nyssa at the table, as always. Farida represented the *London* and *Perth*, but her family had only held the position for one generation. A precarious position to be in. One mistake, and she could lose it. That was probably why she brown-nosed the president at every opportunity.

Nyssa had a plate and cup before her, but she wasn't eating. Her eyes flicked to Tadeo, and she inclined her head. She had that look, the one that said, "We share something, and I'm grateful for your discretion."

Tadeo's mind shrunk from that look, tried to escape the thought of their shared secret. He nodded in return and broke eye contact, heading for the buffet. The reminder of today's mission made him restless—energy surging through him as if he were a charged pulse gun.

The rest of the board members and their families sat clustered at tables beside Nyssa's. Nicolas Gonzalez, representative for the recyc deka, *Seattle,* and Omar's ship, the *Vancouver,* sat with his son and wife sipping a flask, his fair complexion mottled.

"Wow, drunk already and not even first shift?" Omar said, raising his voice.

Tadeo slammed an elbow into Omar's side to shut him up before he started ranting about how much Nic had screwed over the *Vancouver.*

"Watch your mouth, Omar. We're not on six anymore."

"Well, someone should say it."

PARAGON

As they waited in line, Tadeo surveyed the rest of the board members. If the flagship *Paragon* was the beating heart of the fleet, then the dekas were its lifeblood. Each of the ten dekas manufactured something vital to the fleet's survival. And each of the five board members represented the interests of two of the ships.

Nassef Yasin, representative for the *Dubai* and *Moscow*, sat with his family beside Jon Lau, representative for the *Beijing* and *Kyoto*. Nyssa had seemed impressed with how Jon had handled the *Kyoto* incident during the riots—when traitors had airlocked the captain and the entire crew. But Nassef was a wild card.

Tom Nielsen, the fifth board member, sat at his own table with his family, his face a perpetual scowl. Tomas represented the *Oslo* and the *Meso* and constantly raised the quotas on water and food, which led to overworked colonists and messed up population management calculations. Tomas was the real cause of all the shortages. If there was one kak board member, it was Tomas Nielsen.

Tadeo ground his teeth and stepped up to the buffet to grab a plate.

The lights flickered above them, and Tadeo exchanged a worried glance with Omar. The low chatter in the galley ceased.

Then they were plunged into darkness.

CHAPTER FIVE

Tadeo's heart sped up, and his hand went to his pulse gun. He could sense Omar doing the same in the darkness. A few helios went up, and the palm-sized spheres floated beside their owners, casting a yellow glow over drawn faces.

Everyone waited—tense, silent—to see if the bridge crew would trigger the sirens. Was it another emergency lockdown? Another terrorist attack, like the hull breach on six? Everyone here was thinking the same thing—he could see it on their faces.

The seconds ticked by, and when it was clear the emergency sirens weren't going to come on—that this was just another power outage—low conversation started up again.

The lights came back on then, and Tadeo released a breath. Just a power outage. One of many in recent weeks.

"Nicolas!" a female voice shouted. Tadeo took an alarmed step toward the board members' tables at the sudden flurry of activity and loud voices. Farida and Jon Lau appeared in the small crowd, helping Nic Gonzalez up from the floor. The wide man wavered on his feet and slurred something to them. The drunk had passed out in the darkness.

"Dumb kak," Omar said.

Tadeo shook his head and turned back to the buffet. He heaped a plate high with food, filled his cup from the water tank, and took a seat at the table where members of the president's guard sat.

"I owe you one for getting me up here," Omar said. "I was gettin' *real* tired of the food down in guard galley."

It *was* good food. Today they had quin flatbread, carsotts, greens, and tiny square slices of soyad. Only command level got to eat like this. The lower levels mostly ate quin and greens, which was what he and Omar had both been eating before their promotions.

A stocky blond guard, Penta Kiva,

walked up with her food and slid into a chair beside Omar. She was the *Oslo* transfer Omar had vouched for when McGill needed to be replaced.

"Lieutenant Raines," she said, inclining her head respectfully.

"Sergeant." Tadeo stabbed a chunk of soyad with his fork and shoved it into his mouth. The mealy fermented protein fell apart on his tongue, belying its age. Soyad was best eaten fresh—it did not age well in the weeks after it left the *Meso*.

Kiva gave Omar a sidelong glance. "Did you hear what happened?" she asked, keeping her voice low.

"Hey to you, too," Omar said. "What'd you hear?"

"A pregnant tech airlocked herself during night shift."

The saliva dried up in Tadeo's mouth.

"Whoa, what?" Omar asked. "Gotta be the first airlocker on this ship in what, over a year?"

"Nineteen months," Tadeo said. Kiva and Omar both looked at him with surprise, but he kept his face expressionless.

"No one knows why she did it." Kiva continued. "But I bet her pregnancy was defective."

"That's not the only reason," a female voice said.

Tadeo looked up to find Tesmee standing next to their table, plate in one hand, cup in the other. She was staring at Tadeo intently, her eyes bright.

"Oh yeah? What else is there?" Omar asked, leaning toward her. But she didn't take her eyes off Tadeo.

"The airlocker was supposed to abort this morning," Tesmee said. "And she found out her husband died on Soren hours before she did it."

Tadeo's gut twisted like he'd eaten rot-tainted quin. He sniffed and took a sip of water. Tesmee had probably nagged Nyssa until she'd shared the same spare details about Era that the rest of the ship would know by last mess.

"How'd you find that out?" Omar said.

Tesmee gave Tadeo a small smile. "You know. I have my ways."

"Ways," Tadeo echoed.

"Yeah, Tadeo," Omar said. "Girl's got her ways."

Tadeo stared Tesmee down, his expression flat, until she swallowed and averted her eyes.

"I need to eat," she said. "Food's getting cold." She whirled and hurried over to her mother's table to sit. Tadeo watched her go. She'd *seen* him last night with Nyssa—where he never should have been during night shift. Omar looked from Tadeo to Tesmee and back.

"You're an *idiot*." Omar said, rolling his eyes.

Kiva's eyes widened, and she froze, her fork hovering above her plate. Everyone at the table had stopped eating and was watching them now.

"Watch yourself, Sergeant." Tadeo shot him the same flat look he'd given Tesmee. He needed to have a talk with Omar about how to address him in front of others now that they were both up here.

"That girl... she'd do—"

"Do what?" Tadeo asked, his voice a warning Omar didn't receive.

"Do *you*. Man, if she looked at *me* like that..." Omar noticed everyone staring and finally got the hint. He dropped his gaze. "Uh—what I mean to say, sir, is..."

Tadeo released his tight grip on his fork, revealing the deep mark it had left in his palm. He shook his head and went back to eating. Everyone else around the table took that as a cue to start eating again, the moment of tension over.

Kiva snorted, and Omar shot her a glare.

She raised one brow and rolled her eyes. "She's not even *sixteen* yet," she said quietly, clearly trying to escape Tadeo's notice. "Doesn't even have her implant."

"And your point?" Omar asked.

"What is *wrong* with you?" Kiva asked.

"Must be something in the water," Omar said. "After that last shipment from the *Oslo*, man, has it been tasting *bad*."

"Yeah, right," Kiva said. "More like it's these suits, cutting off circulation to your brain. Couldn't your guys on the *Vancouver* make them fit a little better? I bet they've been cutting corners. Probably bribing someone in qual scans."

"Gimme a break," Omar said. "The *Oslo* has one job. One job! And you can't even clean the kak out of the water. You'd stab yourselves to death before you figured out how to thread a needle and make a suit."

"These zippers. Utter junk," Kiva said. "In zero G, kak would just fly out of my pockets."

"Don't blame us for that." Omar shoved more food in his mouth and talked around it. "Blame plastics. The *Dubai*'s been failing qual scans for years."

Kiva scoffed. "They have *not*."

"They have so. Ask anyone in tech. I know people from the *Kyoto*."

"You're so full of it," Kiva said, her voice rising. "You wanna settle this with a game of chips?"

"You're terrible. Why would I even bother playing with you again?"

"If I win, you give me your holovid credits for the month."

"Why would I agree to that?"

"'Cause you're cocky and think you can beat me."

"Fine," Omar said. "I'll play you. And you can sit in the lounge and stare at the wall while I use all your credits up."

Tadeo stabbed at his soyad, scraping his fork loudly across the metal plate, and Omar and Kiva fell silent. Omar might lust after the president's daughter, but clearly he and Kiva were a pair made for Infinity.

Was I like Omar and Kiva—so cavalier about things before the hull breach happened? Or maybe everything had changed since last night. Since he'd airlocked Era and realized one of their own guards had been a traitor.

Chief Petroff showed up then, plate and cup in hand, and sat down a few seats from Tadeo. Talk faded at his arrival. The old man didn't bother to greet any of them, but when he saw Tadeo, his eyes went hard.

"Chief," Kiva asked. "Do you know what that power outage was about?"

The guards stilled, waiting to see if Chief would answer or snap Kiva's head off for talking to him before he'd had his morning mess.

Chief took a bite of food and chewed it slowly. "Same old power core issues as last time. Generator's beat to kak down there. The subs on this ship don't know how to keep anything running."

Tadeo pushed his plate away, his appetite gone. Treason-talking subs. Terrorists in the guard. The ships—old and falling apart. Any threats to the fleet needed to be removed. They had enough to worry about.

Tadeo studied the faces around the table. Were there more traitors here—right now? The chief was from the *Perth*, the mining ship, and his old deka loyalties showed through in the people he promoted. Half the command level guards had been born to specialist parents on the *Perth*. They had the highest death rate of any deka, so everyone who was born there was desperate to get off the ship. It was dangerous work—mining meteors, fixing the equipment, dealing with explosives. Had McGill been from the *Perth*, too?

His gaze went to Omar. He was the only one Tadeo could trust to help him with his investigation.

He stood up and pushed his chair in. Omar looked up questioningly, but Tadeo ignored him and headed over to the corner of the room, toward the hydropods, to wait. He folded his arms and leaned against the wall. The scent of the greens wafted over to him, clearing his head.

Petroff finished his food fast and headed out the door. He gave Tadeo another hard look as he passed. "Better get moving, Raines."

Tadeo nodded and gestured to Omar. He frowned and came over to lean against the wall.

"So what's the mission today?" he asked. "Kiva and I placed bets. She thinks we'll get to stand watch while they try to fix the power core."

"I don't ever stand watch in the power core."

"Oh, right," Omar said. "Gotta protect the heir."

"Sergeant Omar," Tadeo said.

Omar stood straighter on reflex.

"Watch how you address me in front of the rest of the guard," Tadeo said.

His eyes widened. "Okay, man. I mean—Lieutenant."

"We're not on patrol or watch today. You and I have a different mission. Let's go check out some holo gear."

"We're conducting an investigation?" Omar asked.

"Everything about this is need-to-know only," Tadeo said, his voice low. "And you don't need to know yet."

CHAPTER SIX

Zephyr woke to laughter and light. It clashed with the sleep-soaked visions still floating through her mind. Blood. Soren. Era. Grimp.

The Legacy Code. A genetic modification for superimmunity... yet it created broken children—too defective to survive. She shielded her eyes against the light making its way through the crack of her bunk's metal privacy panel. She slept in a top bunk, and the lume bar streamed right through.

Dritan was dead.

The memory of it all slammed into her chest, knocking her breath away. She dropped her head back onto her thin pillow. The girls below continued to laugh, and Zephyr swallowed past the lump in her throat. She grabbed her eyepiece from the shelf inside her bunk and slipped it on. A twist of her wrist activated the small black box connected to it, and the 3D holographic interface appeared. Morning mess was almost over. *Kak.*

Era's grief had been all-consuming last night. She'd been hysterical, ranting about the Defect, saying she wouldn't go through with her abortion... *Oh, no.* Era was scheduled to terminate her pregnancy first shift. Zephyr had to get to her.

She slid open the privacy panel and jumped down. The girls below fell silent as she locked her bunk. There were six halfs to a cubic, and one of her bunkmates, a blonde named Kali, sat below, next to Helice... and Paige, who thank Infinitek, lived in a different cubic. Paige had the look of a sweet girl, someone you could trust, all big eyes and bow lips. And Zephyr *had* trusted her once, until Paige showed her who she really was.

Zephyr kept her face blank as she pulled her suit and boots from her locker and changed. She pocketed her holo gear, then dragged a comb through her long reddish-blond hair, trying to hurry, yet dreading

Era's grief—not sure how she could help ease it.

"Dumb glitch," Paige said.

Zephyr went rigid and raised her eyes.

All three tried to pretend they hadn't just been staring at her, but Helice lifted a hand to her mouth to hide a smile.

Rage lit up Zephyr's chest, and she suppressed it like she always did. They were immature, stuck in caretaker sector mentality—hateful and jealous that Zephyr would captain the *London* someday, and they'd just be stuck here doing boring jobs for the rest of their lives. Better to act above them than engage them. That pissed them off even more. Era was all that mattered right now.

Zephyr gave Paige a condescending smirk, flipped her hair over her shoulder, and left the cubic. When she'd escaped the bunk to the busy corridor beyond, she took deep breaths, holding her head high as she pushed past the milling halfs of singles sector. A group of boys stared at her as she went by, and two of them purposely stepped in her path, nasty expressions on their faces. She pushed past without acknowledging their presence.

Space them all.

She walked quickly through the corridors to the main stairwell and headed down to paired couples sector, weaving her way through the throngs of colonists heading up to mess. The scent of boiled quin wafted down from the galley, turning her stomach.

Most of the colonists she passed were dressed in the green suits of sublevel workers or the black of techs, like Zephyr. A few in light blue suits pushed by—medics. Hopefully Era was still in her cubic and hadn't gone to medlevel alone. People chattered around her, all talking about the same thing.

"An airlocker."

"Down on the sublevels."

Airlocker? A suicide on the ship. And she'd thought security was tighter here. Zephyr pushed the thought from her mind and quickened her pace. As she reached level one, the knots in her stomach rivaled those found in the kak wire shipments the *London* used to get from the *Kyoto*.

This was going to be difficult. After Era's father died, Era had checked out for weeks, listless, crying constantly. Zephyr had tried to comfort her, but Era started going down to the sublevels, and she'd stayed there all day.

She'd brought Zephyr down once to show her why.

Dritan had been so dirty, smelling of the metalworks and sweat, but as soon as Zephyr had seen the way Era looked at him, and the way he protectively cradled her against his chest, she knew Era had found the other half of her infinity.

Now he was dead. And Era and Dritan's unborn child had the Defect. She'd get Era to take more of the grimp. Not enough to get addicted... just enough to numb the pain for the next few days... or weeks.

When Zephyr reached their cubic, she pulled Era's shift card from her pocket, where she'd left it the night before. It was against regulation to have someone else's card, but no one was paying attention to her as she scanned it. The door opened, revealing Era's helio in the darkness. Relief flooded Zephyr, and she stepped inside quickly. The door slid closed behind her.

"Era? Are you...?"

Then she saw who was in the room. Two guards. No Era. The one closest turned toward her, and the helio illuminated his face—his bronze skin, high cheekbones, and the too-long black hair she'd often imagined running her fingers through. "Where's Era? Why are you—"

"Zephyr?" His brows went up, and he took a hesitant step toward her. "How did you get in here?"

The other guard, a dark-skinned man, stepped into their light. He said nothing, just looked from Tadeo to her, and a note of dread rose in her mind, poisoning her earlier relief.

"Where's Era? Where is she?" her voice came out strained.

"Omar, get out," Tadeo said, his voice hard.

"Yes, sir."

Omar gave Zephyr a blank look, then pushed past to exit the cubic.

"Where is Era?" Zephyr repeated. "Is she in trouble?"

Tadeo took a step closer so he towered above her, and Zephyr stumbled back into the wall panel. His face was expressionless, but his brown eyes intense. The yellow glow of the helio made the scene feel wrong, dangerous—like they were trapped together in the depths of the sublevels and not in a paired couples cubic.

"How did you get in here?" Tadeo asked, his voice deep.

"I..."

He noticed the shift card in her hand and lifted it gently, cradling it. Zephyr's skin ignited from the touch, magnetized like the helio floating beside them. They stayed like that for a moment, her hand in his, neither of them taking a breath.

His face darkened. He plucked the card from her grasp and flipped it over, working his jaw as he read Era's name.

"It's against regulation for you to have this."

Zephyr swallowed and dropped her hand to her side, still warm from his touch. "Era dropped it last night. Give it back. I'll make sure she gets it."

"She doesn't need it anymore," he said quietly.

Zephyr's heart beat harder. "Why not?"

"You should leave now." Tadeo averted his eyes, staring at some point beyond Zephyr.

She darted out a hand and rested it on Tadeo's chest, trying to make him look at her. He flinched and grabbed her hand, but didn't push her away.

Instead he met her gaze. "We're conducting an investigation. You can't be here."

"Why? Into what?" Zephyr asked, her voice strong.

His hand tightened around hers. "Era..."

"What? Tell me."

"She airlocked herself during night shift."

Zephyr's breath caught, and she wrenched her hand away from him as if she'd been burned.

"Era committed suicide," Tadeo continued, his voice cold now. He stepped back. "She's dead."

Zephyr let out a little moan and covered her mouth as she fell against the wall panel behind her. She searched Tadeo's face, but it blurred before her. "No. She would never do that—"

"You need to go back to your cubic."

"No," Zephyr said, her voice cracking. "No. She wouldn't do that. Where is she?"

"She did. She's gone, Zephyr."

"How do you even know it was her? It's not—"

"She used her husband's shift card," Tadeo said, his voice flat, his expression unreadable. "She accessed a maintenance airlock and committed suicide."

"You're lying! Is this... is this a sick joke?" Zephyr's throat closed, and she pushed past Tadeo, searching Era's bunk. Empty. No boots. No suit. Her gaze landed on a scrap of pale green cloth on the shelf—exec standard bedding. Zephyr grabbed it and held it to her chest, wavering on her feet. *No.* This felt like a trick, like she was watching a holovid. She had to still be asleep in her bunk.

"It's true." Tadeo's voice sounded like it came to her from the end of a long corridor. "And you need to leave now."

Zephyr whirled to face him, dazed. "It's not possible. She's... She's got to be at medlevel... at—"

"She's gone," he said, his voice pained.

"Did you see her?" Zephyr's voice rose, but she couldn't control it. "I want to see her. I know she wouldn't have..."

"You can't. We didn't... We didn't recover her body."

"Then how do you know it was her? It had to be someone else."

"A transport saw her, and we have her shift card access data."

"Maybe it wasn't her."

Tadeo took a deep breath and stepped closer. He met her eyes, and his were kinder now.

"But it *was* her," he said quietly. "I read it in the report—she lost her husband and had an abort session scheduled today. The last few airlockers had similar reasons."

Zephyr gripped Tadeo's suit, pulling him closer, forcing him to keep his eyes on hers. "She would *not* do this." Her voice broke on the words, and pain surged through her body.

"I'm sorry." His voice came out soft, like he really meant it, like her grief was his own.

Dritan and Era... dead.

"No!" Zephyr slammed her fists into Tadeo's chest, hard. He stumbled back and caught himself on the bunk. Tears filled Zephyr's eyes, and she hit him again and again, until he wrapped her in strong arms and pushed her into the wall.

A strange expression crossed his face, and he grabbed one of her arms, painfully, and shoved her into the corner. He leaned close.

"I'm sorry you lost her," he said, his breath warm against her cheek. "But you need to control yourself."

"Let me go." Zephyr tried to break free, but he squeezed her arm harder. "You're hurting me."

"Do you want to end up on a forced dose of grimp?" Tadeo hissed.

"Era wouldn't do this. I just saw her last night..."

"People commit suicide," he snapped, his voice cold. He pushed her into the wall. "They just do, and no one ever knows why. No one can tell you what she was thinking or why she did it. You just have to accept it. Get over it."

Zephyr's heart raced, and lights danced in front of her. She couldn't breathe. She was going to lose it right here. "I can't—Get off me."

"Get over it, Zephyr. Move on. Airlockers aren't worth getting put on grimp for." Tadeo let go of her and jabbed at the button beside the door. "Now go. We have this handled."

Zephyr clutched Era's scrap of cloth to her chest and pushed past the guard waiting outside. None of this felt real. She was going to wake up soon. This was just a dream.

She ran down the corridor, not seeing the people around her, not hearing them, not feeling their touch as she brushed by them. A molten ball of metal expanded in her chest, and she took quick, small breaths, until spots drifted across her vision.

She made it to the end of the corridor before the pressure in her chest grew unbearable. The air tasted thin and dirty, as if the air recyc had malfunctioned.

Too many people on this ship. Never any privacy. Always people staring at her, getting in her way. She searched for somewhere to go, to be alone, but there was only door after door of paired couples' cubics.

A group of colonists rounded the corner, blocking her path. She squeezed her body against the wall, clutching the blanket to her as they filled the corridor. She gulped back a sob and tried to suck in breath through her tight throat.

One of the women looked at Zephyr and narrowed her eyes at the scrap of illegal exec-standard cloth. Zephyr's gaze dropped to the woman's pregnant belly, and another sob bubbled up in her throat. She slammed herself through the group, continuing her run down the corridor. They shouted something to her, but she turned a corner, seeking refuge.

A crowd of women exited a lav, staring at her wide-eyed. Zephyr squeezed by them, through the doors, and frantically searched for someplace, any place, to be alone. She shut herself in the first vacant shower she found and pressed her back against the wet wall. Drops of water seeped through her suit as she struggled to take breaths.

"No." She slammed her first into the metal stall, and the door shook. Dizzy, hyperventilating, she sunk down onto the wet floor and pressed her face against her arms.

I should have been there. This is my fault. I should have stayed with her. Fucked curfew.

Someone banged on the stall. "Are you alright in there?"

"Go away." Zephyr forced the words out.

Steps receded, leaving Zephyr on her own once more.

The pain in her chest was heavy metal, crushing her, making her light-headed. Era had been her best friend since they were little girls—her only true friend. She wasn't gone. She *couldn't* be gone.

Zephyr sobbed, her muscles cramping, her bones aching with the pain of it. A gaping black hole opened up inside of her, and it threatened to swallow her.

She was suffocating. If she didn't breathe right, she'd pass out. She made herself think of her father—all the times he'd come for her in a rage. When he'd beat her—on her arms, her back, her legs—all the places he could be sure her suit would hide the cuts and bruises. He beat her until she had no emotions—until she'd learned to turn them off.

Zephyr tried to hum between ragged breaths. It was the old song she'd hummed to herself a thousand times before. The song that helped her during all the other times she couldn't breathe.

Her windpipe opened up, and as oxygen returned to her lungs, she whispered the words.

> *They say it's the end.*
> *Can't close my eyes and pretend*
> *Fires haven't burned this place up.*
> *But you and I—we're enough.*
>
> *We'll get through, 'til the day*
> *When this nightmare fades away.*

It was stupid, some ancient song she'd found in her family's files, but it worked. She took in a deep, sputtering breath and stood. Her suit stuck to her, soaked through where it had touched the walls and floor. The pain still twisted deep within her, but now it was buried—unreachable. The numb nothingness would last long enough for her to get back to her bunk.

The ability to switch off her pain was a gift. She'd shut hers off just as surely as if it were a holo and she'd twisted her wrist.

CHAPTER SEVEN

Tadeo stared at the door for a full minute after Zephyr left, clenching and unclenching his fists, his heart beating hard against his chest—just waiting for her to come back, to accuse him of having airlocked Era. But she didn't. Why would she? He sank down on the bunk and hung his head in his hands. He let out a long breath. The grief on her face—he'd recognized it well. It dredged up so much he didn't want to ever feel again.

He'd wanted nothing more than to draw her to him, to hold her and tell her he understood. Because he *did*. He knew what it was like to ask why. Why would anyone choose the shame of airlocking themselves? But being a traitor was a hundred times more shameful.

Zephyr was a command level exec like him—and it was important her reputation not be tied to Era's. There was no way Zephyr was a traitor and no way *she* could have had any idea what Era had been up to. She might hate him now and forever—after how he'd handled this—but it was for the best.

A knock sounded on the door. Omar—probably wondering what was going on. As Tadeo stood, his helio followed his movements, and something on top of the nearly empty shelf reflected the yellow globe. He swallowed hard and took a step nearer, but he knew what it was before his hand closed over the plastic packaging. His pulse quickened. *Grimp.*

He held it up to the light. It was an entire month's worth, though he would have burned through it in a week. The small blue-green pills called to him, reminded him of the bliss they'd deliver the moment they hit his tongue.

Tadeo licked his lips and counted them again. Could he have just one?

He should leave it here. The withdrawal wasn't worth even an hour of bliss.

Another knock sounded on the door, more insistent this time, and Tadeo jumped.

He cleared his throat and jammed the packet into the pocket on his pant leg. He strode over to the door and opened it for Omar.

"What was that about, man? Was that... Zephyr Kerrigan?"

"Yes. She was a friend of the airlocker's."

"You said something about her. Were you two...?"

"We need to finish searching." Tadeo turned away and surveyed the room.

"Uh... Are you sure you're fine?"

"I'm fine," Tadeo snapped.

Omar frowned, but he backed off, like he always did. "So... What's our mission?"

Tadeo worked his jaw and decided to tell him everything—except for Era's involvement. That could come later, when it was time to search the Repository. Infinitek-willing, no one except Nyssa and Chief would ever know what really happened last night.

"Like I told you—this was the airlocker's cubic," Tadeo said. "Her husband got sent to Soren with the first transport."

"He worked with the terrorists?"

"On the same crew. We believe others may be working against us."

Omar's brows went up, and he glanced around at the cubic nervously. "What are we looking for here?"

"Anything that doesn't belong. Something... hidden. Perhaps a data cube."

Another knock sounded, and Omar let the maintenance worker they'd called into the room.

The young sub, her cheek smudged with grease, was carrying a new lume bar. Her eyes widened when she saw Omar and Tadeo by light of the helio. "Sirs. You asked for a lume bar?"

"Yes. Install it now."

She got to work, and Tadeo paced the small cubic, assessing it. Dingy. Not much storage. A tattered blanket lay on the floor next to the double-width bunk. The only storage in the room was the small, empty shelf, and all that was on there now were two canteens and a helio.

Zephyr had grabbed a scrap of exec-level bedding off the shelf, too. He should have taken it from her. Tadeo walked over and picked up the helio. These weren't allowed in personal quarters, so this one had likely been stolen from the sublevels. He shook his head.

PARAGON

Black market trading, maybe. They'd seen it before. It happened on every ship—and the penalty was harsh. If colonists were caught with illegal resources, they were beaten with the rod and assigned strict rations for a month. But an illegally obtained helio was hardly evidence of terrorism or treason.

The sub finished installing the lume bar, and the room lit up with its harsh light. Tadeo deactivated his helio and hooked it to his belt as the worker climbed down off the bunk.

"Sub," Tadeo said. "What's your name?"

"Gemma, sir. Gemma Kian."

"Are any of the panels screwed or riveted on in here?"

"Yes, sir. Plenty. But the ones along that wall pop off on their own," she said, pointing near the door.

"You're going to help us take off every panel in here. Everything will be removed."

"Yes, sir." Her shoulders slumped beneath his scrutiny.

"And, *Gemma*, if you tell anyone what you do or see here, you'll find yourself taking a trip to Soren. Understand?"

"Yes... yes, sir. I'll go get my tools." She disappeared out the door.

Omar whistled. "Were they always that obedient? Shoulda started sending 'em down to Soren earlier."

Tadeo grunted a non-committal response and worked his fingers beneath the first removable panel. The connectors made a popping sound as they released, and Omar helped him lower the metal slab to the floor.

Tadeo pushed aside the tangled wires and components beneath, but nothing looked unusual. There was certainly no archive cube hidden here.

As he and Omar took off the rest of the panels, moving around wires to try to catch a glimpse of anything out of place, he tried not to think of what had happened in this cubic last night. Or of the drugs pressed against this leg that could help him forget.

Gemma returned and began the slow process of removing screws from the permanent panels. Tadeo checked the space between the walls, but in each instance, they found nothing. Midmess was approaching when she finished removing the last wall panel and stepped up on the bunk to start on the ceiling.

"Sirs? This one looks like... like it's loose." She pulled on the panel, and screws clattered to the floor and smacked off the metal sheets they'd removed.

"Take it down." Tadeo's heart sped up, and he pushed off the wall he'd been leaning against as he waited.

The girl moved out of his way as he hopped up on the bunk. He activated his helio again and used it to cast light into the narrow ceiling space above. A bundle of wires were tied off up there, and a thin pipe ran across the middle of the space.

There. The helio moved with Tadeo, and metal glinted. Something shiny had been jammed far back in the space. He reached his hand in and felt for it, gently pulling at it to see if it would come away. Sharp edges, solid metal. Another tug, and the piece came away in his grasp.

Tadeo pulled the object out, and something fell off the top of it, tumbling onto the bunk.

He peered down at the heavy metal rectangle in his hands. It was longer than both his hands, etched with circuitry, and had a series of square indentations. He had no idea what it could be, but it didn't belong up in the ceiling, loose like that.

"What is that?" Omar asked.

Tadeo jumped down from the bunk and snatched up the object that had fallen off the metal rectangle. It was a very old shift card. He could tell by the web of cracks covering the plastic. He turned it over. A helix and a three-sided symbol—the triquetra—were printed on the other side. The medlevel symbol. What was Era... or Dritan... doing with a medlevel shift card?

He held up the metal rectangle. "Do either of you know what this is?"

Gemma nodded. "I do." She took it from Tadeo and turned it over in her hands. "Belongs in recyc. Look here," she said, pointing to a jagged edge. "It has an odd edge, like someone took a welding tool to it."

"So what *is* it?"

Gemma's brow furrowed, and she looked from Tadeo to Omar with confusion. "Well... it's a power cell. They're all over the ship. In every cubic, they store back-up power for lockdowns or outages. But this one's empty, see?" She pointed at the square indents. "Power strips go here. This one's used up."

Tadeo's mind raced. "Where are they in the cubics?"

Gemma walked over to the door and

tore off the panel Tadeo and Omar had checked first. She made a little noise.

"Needs new wiring in here," she said, almost to herself. She drove her hand down into the panel and lifted out the insert. Bright yellow strips lined the indentations. "See? This one's still good."

"And where do they go when they're used up?"

Gemma cocked her head at him, like she was surprised at the question. "To recyc. Then back to the power deka. They charge them on the *Beijing*."

"Can we trace this, find out where it's been?"

"No. They're interchangeable—no unique ID numbers."

Tadeo shook his head and glanced down at the cracked medlevel card still in his hand. Alone, the piece of recyc might be another bit of black market contraband... but *with* the medlevel card and hidden in the ceiling? No. Something was off here.

"Omar, finish searching here and get this cubic back together. When you're done, comm me for instructions."

"Got it. Sir."

Midmess buzzer rang as Tadeo exited the cubic, still clutching the medlevel card in hand. This card had belonged to someone, and he was going to find out who—and why it had been hidden in the Corinth cubic. He hurried for the main stairwell. Colonists moved out of his way, but even then, it still took nearly a half hour for him to reach level four through the crush of the midmess crowd.

He hesitated when he reached the medlevel doors. He avoided this place as much as possible—but today he had no choice. He forced himself to enter the waiting area. High metal counters lined the walls, and clerks wearing holo gear stood behind each one. They worked with the bulky black boxes atop each counter, the stationaries, checking patients in. Tadeo went to the back of the area, to the station marked *Records*. The three colonists waiting in line stepped out of his way when they saw him and stared as he stepped up to the counter.

"Go back to your seats," Tadeo said.

They all quickly backed away, taking seats at the nearest bench.

The clerk behind the records counter licked his lips, then glanced around, as if he wanted to escape and not be the one to deal with a guard. He twisted his wrist, shutting off his reflective eyepiece. The glasstex cleared.

"Yes, sir? How can I help you?"

Tadeo slid the shift card across the counter toward him. "I want to know whose card this is."

The man picked up the card and scanned it against a flat gray scanpad hooked to the stationary. "No data. No record. The card doesn't even exist. Must be an old one that got stripped and sent to recyc."

"I need you to figure out who it used to belong to then," Tadeo said.

The young man looked behind him, where an older black-suited tech sat on a bench against the wall, working on holo gear in his lap. "Day, will you come look at this? He needs to find out who owned it, but we have no record on it."

Day got up and came over to the counter. "No number at all? Strange." He peered down at the card. "They had these when I was a half—twenty years back. Old-style shift cards made on *Dubai*."

"Then it should be easy to figure out whose this was, shouldn't it?" Tadeo asked.

eyepiece darkened. He gestured in the air, accessing patient files on a 3D interface only he could see.

"Names?"

"Dritan Corinth and Era Corinth. Put all their records on the cube."

"Anything else, sir?"

"I also want full patient records on Samuel Smith, Tatiana Carizo, and Jonas Keen."

The young clerk's mouth dropped open. He no doubt recognized the names of the three terrorists who had just been airlocked. He licked his lips and gestured for a few more minutes, then popped the cube out of the stationary.

"Here you go." His voice cracked. He cleared his throat. "Anything else?"

"This is a confidential investigation." Tadeo lowered his voice. "If you tell anyone about this data pull, you'll find yourself in the brig. Or worse."

The man held up his hands. "I understand."

Tadeo took the cube and strode to the corner of the waiting area. He chose an empty bench against the wall and pulled his holo gear out of his pocket. He put on the eyepiece and pushed the cube into the handheld's slot, then activated it with a twist of his wrist.

The Infinitek logo, an infinity symbol, twisted in the air before him and faded into the mantra of the fleet.

A Better World Awaits.

Then five files appeared, the traitors' names beneath each of them. He selected Dritan's.

> *Dritan Corinth;*
> *Sub-level maintenance*
>
> *MedBay: Physical*
> *Transfer from the London :*
> *Physical Results: Good health*
>
> *MedBay: Injuries*
> *Second-degree burn*
> *Follow-up:*
> *Healed and cleared for sublevel work*

Dritan had seen two different medics in his ten months aboard the *Paragon*. Nothing strange noted. Tadeo opened Era's files next.

PARAGON

Era Corinth; Repository Tech

MedBay: Physical
Transfer from the London:
Physical Results: Good health

MedBay: Population Management
Implant removal
Pregnancy test - Positive
Follow-up – Genscanning
Canceled, amniocentesis performed
Follow-up - Pregnancy defective

The final date was flagged, and Tadeo's stomach churned as he read it.

Termination Procedure
Appointment missed

Tadeo closed out Era's records. Nothing strange mentioned on them, but he made note of the medic she'd been scheduled to see for her last three appointments—Medic Nora Faust.

Sam, Tatiana, and Jonas had all arrived ten months ago, during the same transfer period as Dritan and Era. He combed through their records next. All of them had the standard physical exams as well as several follow-up exams for minor sublevel work injuries.

When he reached the end of Tatiana's record, his eyes caught a flagged item. He tapped it.

> *Tatiana Carizo;*
> *Sub-level maintenance*
>
> *MedBay: Population Management*
> *Annual Implant Renewal*
>
> *Note: Patient arrived for yearly implant renewal complaining of pain from termination procedure performed on the Meso one year prior. Patient refused procedure and demanded consult with Medic Nora Faust. When Medic Faust was not immediately called in, patient grew angry, striking out at Medic Meletsky. Medic Faust brought in to perform patient's implant renewal procedure, and patient was started on 80mg grimp.*

Tadeo deactivated the holo gear, and his pulse quickened. Why had Tatiana asked for Medic Faust, specifically, by name like that? Medic Faust had also treated Era. Could there be a connection?

CHAPTER EIGHT

Tadeo's commcuff buzzed, and Omar's ID popped up. Tadeo stood and walked to the edge of the waiting area, away from anyone who might overhear.

He answered the comm. "Raines."

"We're done in the airlocker's cubic," Omar said, his voice thin, tinny through the ancient earbud in Tadeo's ear. "Found nothing else. Where do you want me next?"

"When you looked through the terrorists' cubics in singles sector," Tadeo said, "you didn't allow maintenance workers in, did you?"

"No—only guards. But we did a clean sweep."

"Is it possible you missed any attached panels?"

Omar paused. "Maybe? We didn't rip the whole cubic apart to bare metal like this."

"Bring the power cell insert to my locker on six, grab something to eat from mess, then head back down to singles sector with Gemma," Tadeo said, keeping his voice low. "I want you two to tear apart the terrorists' bunks again. Every single place in the wall, ceiling, and floor. Just to be sure nothing was missed. I'll meet you there soon."

"Yes, sir."

Tadeo turned off his commcuff. It would take the records tech hours to figure out who that medlevel card may have belonged to. Omar's search would likely turn up nothing, and then they needed to search the Repository, which could take days. So while he was still on medlevel, he'd follow up on this connection between Era, Tatiana, and Medic Faust.

He headed over to the population management station.

A brunette clerk gestured, engrossed in her holo screen. "I have an appointment during the morning shift," she said to the patient in front of her.

"Excuse me," Tadeo stepped up to the station.

The girl's head jerked toward him in surprise. "Can I help you, sir?"

"I need to see Medic Faust."

Her hand tightened into a fist mid-air. "Nora Faust is no longer a medic."

"What do you mean?"

"She has power core sickness. She's in hospice."

"What room?"

The girl pressed her lips together and performed a series of hand gestures. "Hospice MedBay D, Bed 124."

Tadeo turned and headed for the back of the waiting area. The glass doors slid open, and he forced himself to pass into the wide corridor beyond. The sharp, sickly-sweet mix of cleaning solution and power-core sickness drugs made him break out in an immediate sweat and sent a wave of nausea through him. He breathed through his mouth and focused on the metal triquetra and double-helix symbol engraved on a panel at the end of corridor. Medics in light blue suits bustled around him, heading deep into the level.

His mind went to the grimp in his pocket— and to the fact that he could get high for the rest of his life off the stash they had on med-level.

When he'd been coming off grimp on the *Meso*, his mother closed down the command level medcubic under the pretense of repairs, and one medic watched over him every shift until the grimp was out of his system.

The bone-deep pain, the hallucinations, the sweating and vomiting—it was unbearable. But then the grief returned along with the rest of his emotions. Dealing with his pain over Kit was the worst part of the withdrawal.

After Kit died, his mother was there for him every hour of every day. She *saved* him. She somehow managed to run the ship and nurse him through his grimp addiction, then through his grief. She was his strength when he had none.

He was sixteen when Kit died, beyond the caretaker sector mentality of desiring to be coddled by a mother or by anyone else. But he loved Kit, and she airlocked herself because of him. There was nothing worse than that.

As he came down off the grimp, all the grief rooted within him bloomed into something fierce and terrible. His mother held him and talked him through it, made him see the truth.

"She made her own choices," his mother said. "Both of you did. And her last choice was hers and hers alone. Some of us simply don't have the genes needed to bear this burden. Some can't handle the pressure of doing their part in this fleet—of living selflessly to ensure humanity makes it to New Earth."

"This was my fault," Tadeo said.

"No. Kit chose this. Not everyone can see the truth—that the darkness of space will end someday. And that the end of our darkness will be our new beginning. It could be just on the other side of the next jump. The survival of the human race depends on colonists who believe in that and have enough faith to do what's needed to get there. Kit didn't have that faith."

He felt betrayed when she said it, as if Kit hadn't deserved to live. "The fleet's not *better off* without her."

His mother gripped his hand tight. "You may have made mistakes, but you get to live and make new choices. Will you dedicate your life to this fleet—to leading your ship? Or will you let her choices and mistakes destroy you both? I know what you're made of. I know

Day let out a surprised laugh, and Tadeo shot him a glare.

Day paled. "There are thousands of med-level workers this could've belonged to."

"Well, then, you," Tadeo said, pointing to Day, "will find out when this card was manufactured, then go make a list of every person it *may* have belonged to since."

Day looked at the floor. "Yes, sir." He moved to an empty counter beside them and logged into the system, apparently getting to work.

Tadeo shook his head, frustrated at the dead-end lead. Omar was finishing up in Era's cubic, and then they'd begin the very long process of searching the Repository. Tadeo had time to pull records—see if Dritan, Era, or any of the terrorists Dritan had been involved with, had done anything suspicious on med-level. Maybe there'd be a hint as to how the Corinths ended up with that card.

Tadeo took the blank data storage cube from the pocket where he'd stored his holo gear and handed it to the clerk. "Now I need some records."

The clerk inserted the small metal cube into the stationary and twisted his wrist. His what this family's made of. We're strong. The Raines family never quits."

He got angry at that—punched a dent in a wall panel and injured his hand. But his mother was right. Kit killed herself. She'd quit. In the end, he'd decided to survive. And to lead.

Tadeo kept his eyes on the words engraved above each corridor he passed.

Population Management.

Physicals.

Injuries.

Hospice.

He turned down the hospice corridor. Half the level was dedicated to the dying. He reached medbay D and stepped into the vast, dimly lit space.

A young medic got up from a chair near the door. "Can I help you?" she asked in a quiet voice.

"Yes. I need to speak to Nora Faust in bed 124."

"Right this way."

She led him past dozens of cots, each with thin curtain barriers between them. Most had the curtains drawn for privacy, but the patients he could see were hooked up to machines, sleeping or staring into nothing with glazed eyes.

Some people chose to die on their own ships when the power core sickness came for them, but many chose to die with the comfort of an unending supply of drugs in *Paragon*'s hospice bays. Core sickness spared no one. For an entire lifetime, the power cores radiated every colonist's cells. Their superimmunity—a gift of the Legacy Code—kept the radiation at bay for only so long. Eventually, the immune system turned on itself, confused, overzealous, attacking the very body it was supposed to protect. Tadeo didn't want to go out like that.

They reached bed 124. An old woman with short gray hair lay in the bed, a white sheet pulled up around her. Tadeo shifted on his feet and glanced back toward the exit. There was no way this dying woman was any kind of lead. He'd made a mistake coming here.

As the medic set up a chair beside the bed, Nora's eyes opened.

"Medic," Tadeo said. "Can you turn on that light?" He gestured to the lume bar above Nora's cot.

"Yes, sir. I can from the front of the bay." The medic drew the curtains, and the sound of her boots on the tile floor receded.

It was even darker with the curtains drawn. Tadeo took a seat, but the space was so small, his knees brushed the cot. Nora Faust sat up, flapping impatiently at the wires attached to her chest. They connected to a metallic disc and led to the life monitoring box beneath the cot. The metal machine beeped lowly in the silence, joining the chaotic hum of the other machines in the bay.

"I get the pleasure of a guard visit?" Nora asked. "Welcome to my new cubic." She pursed her lips and gestured around at the curtains, then pointed to the canteen next to her cot. "I'd offer you a drink, but the water tastes like it came from the kak in recyc. The dying don't need to drink clean. Policy, you know."

Her gray hair reminded him of the streaks of gray in his own mother's hair. She was getting up in age... in her forties now. Most people didn't go to hospice until after they turned fifty, but some died younger. Guilt tugged at Tadeo. He needed to visit the *Meso*.

Tadeo coughed and crossed his arms.

"You don't look like you belong here."

Nora sniffed. "If they keep drugging me up, I will."

"When were you diagnosed?"

"Two days ago. They took me off my shifts. I should still be working. It hasn't progressed much yet."

"In population management, correct?"

"What is this about?" Nora sighed and looked at the curtains like she wanted to escape. "Shouldn't you be guarding someone on command level or something? We had terrorists on this ship, you know."

Tadeo stiffened and tightened his fists. What was wrong with this woman? She talked like a disrespectful sublevel half. "I have a few questions to ask you."

The lume bar above the cot finally flickered on, and Tadeo squinted against the sudden bright light.

Nora leaned over the cot, peering at him, and stopped a few inches from his face. "Who did you say you were again?"

"Lieutenant Raines. I'm on the president's personal guard. Now—"

"*Tadeo* Raines?" Her eyebrows leapt upward, and her hand darted out to touch his face.

Tadeo pushed her hand away and jerked back against his chair. You did *not* touch a guard like that. Ever. But this woman was old and dying, and he needed to get this over with so he could move on to the Repository. "Ma'am, I just have a few questions to ask about some of your patients."

Nora laughed and crossed her arms. "You look just like your mother."

Tadeo stilled. "Excuse me?"

"What did you want to know about my patients?"

His mother? How did this medic know anything about his mother? "Are you from the *Meso*?"

Nora's expression hardened. "No. I've been here my entire life."

"Then how..." Tadeo shook his head. He didn't have time for this. He activated his handheld and started the audio recording program. "We're beginning the interview now. Please state your name."

"Nora Faust."

"Nora, did you see a patient named Tatiana Carizo?"

Nora stared at Tadeo for one long moment,

then licked her lips. "Hmm. Name doesn't sound familiar."

"Really? Interesting. We just airlocked her for treason. I thought every person on this ship knew Tatiana's name."

"How unfortunate." A small smile appeared on Nora's lips. "No. I can't remember ever treating her."

She was lying. Tadeo was sure of it. But *why?* "Tatiana's file says she assaulted Medic Meletsky. I'm surprised it wasn't reported to the guards. Tatiana should have been thrown into the brig. But instead, she asked for you—by name, and you stepped in to talk to her. What did she say to you?"

"Can't remember." Medic Faust tapped her head with two fingers and met his gaze. "It's these core sickness drugs. They addle the mind."

"Tatiana came in for a routine implant renewal and complained of pain from a recent termination. *You* talked to her."

"I do renewals all the time."

"I need to know what she said."

"I suppose she said she was in pain," Nora snapped. "You have the file. Stop asking stupid questions."

For a moment, Tadeo was too shocked to reply. Who did this woman think she was?

"Tatiana was a terrorist," Tadeo said through gritted teeth. "We need to know what she said to you."

"I have no recollection."

"Were you supposed to terminate Era Corinth's pregnancy this morning?"

"Yes."

"Tell me what *she* said to you during your examinations."

Nora considered Tadeo, sweeping her gaze from the top of his head down his uniform. "No. I don't think I will."

Tadeo's face heated, and he forced himself to unclench his fists. "You're refusing to answer the question?"

"Era said nothing unusual."

Tadeo took a breath and leaned back in his seat. "Do you know what Era did last night shift?"

"What is this about? I'm done answering questions, and I need rest." Nora looked through the crack in the curtains. "Medic!"

"Era airlocked herself last night."

Nora's hand went to her chest. "What?"

Tadeo kept his gaze on her, unblinking. "Maybe you know why she did it. She must have said something to you."

She clutched the sheet, twisting it in her grasp. Then she closed her eyes and settled her head back onto the pillow.

"I'm conducting an investigation," Tadeo said. "Do you know something about Era and Tatiana? Were they working together?"

Nora didn't open her eyes. "Go away."

"Sit up."

She didn't move.

"Sit up and answer my question."

Nora rolled away from him.

Hot anger lit up in Tadeo's chest, and he leaned over the bed to haul Nora into a sitting position. Her arms were icy cold. She was so thin, so frail.

She opened her eyes, and there were tears in them. "Do you think I don't feel every death? I do," she said, her voice hard. "You're a *Raines*. If you want answers to your questions, ask your traitorous mother. Now get your hands off of me."

Tadeo froze, his hands still clutching her arms, and she pulled away from him. He sank back into the chair, his heart pounding. *My traitorous mother?*

"My *mother* is the most loyal captain in the fleet—and a model *every* captain should follow," he said, his voice low, threatening.

Nora narrowed tear-filled eyes at him. "I was around long before you, *boy*."

"You don't talk about the captain of the *Meso* that way," he said roughly.

"How about the son?" She wiped at her eyes. "You've followed right in your mother's footsteps. You're both a curse on this fleet."

Tadeo balled his hands into fists and stood. "Will you or will you not answer the questions I've asked you?"

"I will not."

"You realize what this looks like—that you're protecting a known terrorist?"

"I'm dying. I don't give a kak."

"I'm sure the president will."

"Perhaps you ought to interview her, then. Especially if you're looking for terrorists."

"Now, *you're* speaking treason." Tadeo worked his jaw and glanced toward the thin curtain barrier between Medic Faust's bed and the next. *Fuck.* His damn handheld had recorded all of this, including her accusations of his own mother being a traitor. He twisted his wrist to shut it off.

Nora watched him do it, and a slight smile spread on her lips, as if she dared him to hand the recording over to Chief now.

Tadeo's comcuff buzzed. He shot Nora a threatening glare and answered it. "What?"

"We found something," Omar said. "You gotta get down here, now."

"I'll comm you right back."

Tadeo switched off his cuff and pointed at Medic Faust. "You are obstructing an ongoing investigation. I'm not done with you yet."

She glared back at him without responding, and he shoved aside the curtain and strode out of the medbay, his mind racing. Nora Faust seemed to hate his mother *and* the president, but it was hard to believe this dying medic could have worked here her whole life and suddenly become involved with terrorists.

Still, she was hiding something. And she could spend some time in the brig until she decided to tell him what Tatiana and Era had said during their visits.

As he made his way down medlevel's corridors toward the main stairwell, he commed the brig.

"Lieutenant Raines here. Please send two guards to medlevel immediately to transfer Nora Faust to the brig."

"Where is the colonist, sir?"

"Medbay D, Bed 124."

"Sir... hospice?"

"Arrest her," Tadeo said.

He disconnected and commed Omar.

"What did you find?"

"We found a canister of explosives," Omar said, his voice strained. "And it's empty."

CHAPTER NINE

Dritan limped around the pile of crushed corpses, searching for any sign of extra supplies. He found a space between a body and rock and worked his hand beneath the boulder, feeling around for the belt he knew would be there.

His forearm slid along a slick surface, blood and guts, and his stomach lurched. He swallowed back the urge to puke up the vacuum-packed quin bar he'd just eaten. His hand closed around a belt, and he gripped the edges of two oxygen packs and dragged them out, slowly. He'd lost one already to a sharp rock.

He breathed easier as the packs came out intact. He crawled over the rock with his haul, his injured arm aching from exertion, until his helio's light cast its glow on Jan.

She looked asleep, listless, her skin deathly pale beneath her oxygen mask. Her chest seemed to barely rise and fall with each breath. Dritan's chest tightened at the sight of the puddle of blood beneath her trapped leg. It had slowly grown in size in the past few hours, evidence of how much she'd lost.

"Jan." He laid the quin bars and oxygen packs beside her, next to the medkit he'd found. He shook her, and she opened her eyes. "I found more oxygen."

She blinked at the light of the helio and looked around, dazed. Then her unfocused eyes found his again. "How many... how many packs left?"

"Two. We have enough for another twelve hours, at most. I'm sorry—I didn't find another medkit. We're out of painmod."

Jan's blue eyes shone. "Doesn't matter. The truth is... I can't feel much of anything anymore."

Dritan's throat thickened. "Just hang in there, okay?"

"Earlier... I thought I heard a voice... from there," Jan said. She lifted one limp arm, pointing toward a crevice near her. It was the same spot where the crew had been working to remove rubble before the quake killed them.

"I would've heard it," Dritan said. She was delusional, hallucinating from blood loss.

"You need to check."

"Listen," Dritan said, kneeling next to her, closer. "I'm going to leave again—try to find more water and oxygen—"

"You know, I've been thinking about it," Jan said. "In the tube we descended when we got here... they must have had an air recyc fan in there."

Dritan sat up straighter. "What do you mean?"

Jan groaned and let her head rest on the rock wall behind her. "On meteors. When I was on the *Perth*. The staging sites always have a recyc fan filled with extra packs."

Dritan swallowed. "Even if there was a fan... I can't get to the exit, let alone the tube we came down. If the tube is even still there after the explosion. I'm sorry."

Jan blinked, and he saw the tears in her eyes. "I know."

"They'll come for us. Rescue will come." But the more hours that passed, the less Dritan believed it. Would they come? What if Jan was right? That the president wanted them all dead? Dritan took a quin bar from his belt and handed it to her. "Here. Eat this."

Jan grabbed his sleeve, not taking the bar. "I need to talk to you."

Dritan settled beside her, and as he did, he unwrapped the bar for her.

"I'm not getting out of here," she said.

Dritan met her gaze. "We're not quitting. This isn't over yet. Don't think like that."

She laughed, but it sounded bitter. "All I've been doing is thinking. About my husband—Gavin. And my daughter, Bella. She's only three."

Dritan had been doing everything in his power to push away thoughts of Era. Of their unborn child. "They're safe up there, Jan—"

"No, listen. It's not that. Bell made me promise her I'd take her to Observation and point to the subcity where I'd worked." Jan's voice cracked, but she smiled. "You know... she'd be sad every morning when I'd drop her off at caretaker, so I'd tell her, 'Mama always comes back.' She used to be so happy to see me when I'd pick her up. She'd squeal 'mama' in her little voice and run for me. And every single day, she'd say, 'You always come back.' But... not this time—"

"You will," Dritan said, squeezing her arm. "You'll take Bell up to Observation, and you'll point to this damn kakhole of a planet and tell her you kicked its ass. And then we'll finish the jumpgate. And before she's even a half, we'll jump the fleet. Maybe find New Earth."

Jan's pale blue eyes sparkled with tears in the light of the helio. "Promise me—if you get out of here—you'll look out for my family."

Dritan's throat tightened as he placed half the quin bar in her hand. "Stop it. We're both getting out of here."

"Please."

Dritan forced himself to take a bite of the bar. "Only if you eat. You need to keep up your strength."

Jan's eyes grew even sadder, and she glanced at the pool of blood beneath her leg. But she nodded and took a bite of the bar. "Now you have to promise me."

"Okay," Dritan said. "I swear. But you have to promise *me* that if you're the one who gets out of here, you take care of Era."

"I will. I promise. But if I don't make it..." She reached a shaking hand up to the zipper of her suit and pulled it down, revealing a necklace with a bit of recyc metal hanging from it. "Bring this back to my family for me. Give it to Gavin for Bell. Don't let 'em incinerate it. It's been passed down through Gavin's family for a long time."

"I will. But we're both getting out of here," Dritan repeated. He passed Jan the canteen to wash away the dry taste of the bar.

As she took a drink, a low sound echoed through the cavern. A *voice*. They both froze, exchanging glances.

"Did you—?"

"I heard it," Dritan said. He stood up and took a few steps, listening. Another sound... coming from the crevice. Dritan's pulse quickened, and he stumbled around debris to get to the spot. The opening was pitch dark.

He leaned into it. "Is someone over there?" he called.

"Yes!" A deep, male voice came back.

"I hear you!" Dritan yelled. Hope lifted him, cleared his mind. Another survivor. Jan *hadn't* been hallucinating. And there had to be a gap in the rocks. Otherwise he wouldn't be able to hear the man so clearly. Maybe Dritan could squeeze through there to the other side.

Dritan went back to Jan and dropped one of the oxygen packs beside her. "Guess I should have listened to you. I'm going to try to crawl through."

"Get through." Jan gave him a small, sad smile, visible through her clear mask. "Get yourself out of here."

Dritan leaned forward and smoothed her blood-matted hair out of her face. He looked in her eyes. "We're both getting out of here. You'll see Gavin and Bell. And I'll see Era."

She stared at him for a long moment, then smiled. "A better world awaits."

"And we're gonna get there," Dritan finished.

He handed her another quin bar and left her with an emergency glow to see with, then tightened his mask's strap and crawled around the rocks back toward the crevice, wincing as his injured arm struck rock.

The crevice was a dark gap between the cavern wall and the place the ceiling had fallen in. He hadn't wanted to shove his body through any of these sections earlier, but now he had hope—proof there was something beyond here.

"You still there?" he asked into the darkness.

"I'm here."

"I'm gonna try to come to you." Dritan snatched his helio from the air and placed it snugly in his suit pocket. Then he activated his last glow bar and hooked it to his pocket to help light the way.

Before he could change his mind, he wedged his body into the crevice and gritted his teeth as the rock scraped his arm. The rocks pushed against his chest, icy cold, and his suit stuck to the sweat on his back. Each jutting rock stabbed him like the rivets that lined the tight sections of the sublevel pipes. He tried to pretend he was doing routine maintenance in the sublevels, but without the ever-present deep thrum of the power core, he couldn't convince himself he was anywhere but buried hundreds of feet under solid rock.

He forced himself to take even breaths, but sweat broke out on his brow, and the space grew tighter as he pushed toward the other survivor. If a quake happened now, this might be it for him.

"I see your glow," the man said. He sounded close, only feet away.

"Is there space for me to get through?" Dritan asked, panting.

He heard the sound of rocks moving, hitting the floor, of scree falling. Then a light. A helio. Dritan breathed harder, shoving himself through the tight space.

The globe grew closer, and a few feet later, he reached the edge. He deflated his chest and got through, tumbling onto the ground, crying out as his arm hit the hard stone floor.

He blinked against the helio's light, and a thrill ran through him at the sight of the high ceiling there. This had to be the main cavern where they'd come in.

"I thought I was the only one left," the man said.

Dritan sat up and looked toward the source of the voice, toward the helio. A man sat propped up beside the crevice Dritan had just come from. His leg was bloody, tied up with a messy bandage. Dritan moved closer to the man, and as he did, he made out the face beneath the mask. Dark hair, dark eyes, skin even paler than Jan's. The man was a decade older than Dritan—maybe in his thirties.

It was Bran McGill.

McGill was the *Paragon* guard who had been sent down here with them. The man had acted bitter, never talking to any of them. He'd been kicked out of the guard after Sam had grabbed his pulse gun and used it to threaten the president's daughter. *Sam.* Dritan's gut twisted, and he pushed away memories of his crew. He had to focus. McGill had been here in the main cavern longer—he might know where to find the exit.

"McGill."

McGill leaned forward, peering at him, and his eyebrows shot into his hairline. "Corinth." He let out a low laugh. "The snitch survives."

Dritan went still, his heart in his throat. If any of the subs ever found out what he'd done, he'd be cast out—or worse. The sublevels had their own justice. He jerked forward, slamming his good hand into McGill's chest. "*What did you say?*"

McGill blinked, his expression flat. "Gonna kill me for sayin' the truth? I'm dead anyway. We both are." He swept his hand toward the rest of cavern. "And anyone who might have given a kak about what you did is dead, too."

Dritan held his gaze for a moment longer, then pushed away, getting to his feet.

PARAGON

Every small movement sent a shot of burning pain through his arm, and he cradled it against his body.

All his anger faded away as he made out the shapes along the wall. A pile of boulders sat atop a jumble of crushed bodies, limbs askew. Dritan's stomach turned. It was gruesome, blood splattered along rock, dismembered limbs scattered across the floor. He fought back nausea and turned to McGill.

"We're not the only survivors," Dritan said. "There's another one on the other side. Janet Lanar. She's trapped."

"I hope you aren't wasting oxygen on her," McGill said.

Dritan's nostrils flared. "Do you know the way out of here or not?"

"The few who survived thought the corridor was there," McGill said, pointing to the far wall, near the biggest pile of buried bodies and limbs. "Then the last quake took 'em all out."

The heavy weight in Dritan's chest lightened, despite the scene before him. "We need to clear the rocks, then. Keep working on what they started."

McGill shook his head. "Then what? We came down a fucking tube to get here. You gonna climb to the surface? One breath of Soren air, and we're dead."

"Jan said there might be an air recyc fan there—with extra oxygen packs."

For a moment, McGill looked almost hopeful. But then his expression darkened. "No. More like the entire corridor is gone and the fan with it."

Dritan leaned into the crevice. "Jan," he called out. "Can you hear me?"

A weak cry came back. "Yes."

"I found someone. We're going to try to get to the corridor!"

Another reply came back, but he couldn't make it out.

He looked back at McGill. "Can you walk?"

"Haven't tried lately and don't wanna. I've got just enough painmod to last me till my oxygen runs out." McGill pulled something into the light. A medkit.

Dritan ripped it away from him and opened it. He pulled a painmod syringe from the case. Jan couldn't feel her pain anymore, and if Dritan was going to move rocks, he needed to dull the pain in his arm.

"Give it back." McGill leaned forward, and Dritan snatched the medkit farther away.

"Shut up." Dritan prepped the painmod syringe and plunged the needle into his vein. He sucked in a breath as warmth spread through his arm from shoulder to fingertips.

"We aren't getting out of here. So don't even bother," McGill said.

Dritan ignored him and stood up, stretching his arm as the painmod got to work, and the burning pain faded away. The numb feeling in his arm was blissful, but it wouldn't last long. And there were only seven painmod syringes left.

"We are not dying down here." Dritan said it like it was true. Because it had to be. He wanted to believe it. Had to believe it. Era needed him. Their *child* needed him... If the pregnancy wasn't defective.

"It's been two days." McGill said tonelessly. "It's over. They're not coming."

"Someone will come back here," Dritan said. "Even if they think we're dead, they'll come back. We just need to survive. When did you last take the painmod?"

"A couple hours ago. The numbness will wear off soon enough."

Dritan picked up the medkit with his good arm. "Get up. And show me where the corridor was."

McGill glared at him. "Are you a half-wit? No one is coming," he said, drawing each word out. "Don't you get that?"

"You wanna die down here? Fine. But I'm getting to that recyc fan. And Jan and I will still be alive when rescue comes."

McGill's expression smoothed into something unreadable. He studied Dritan for a minute, then finally held out a hand so Dritan could help him to his feet.

"Now show me exactly where they thought the corridor was," Dritan said.

The two of them limped around rocks and bodies, McGill leading them to the spot where they'd been digging. McGill's leg didn't look right, but he didn't complain.

When they reached the spot, Dritan released him and took in the wall of rubble. It extended halfway to the ceiling, a mixture of immovable boulders and scree. He lowered the medkit to the ground and checked his oxygen. Half-full.

He chose the smallest rock from the rubble, and tried to heft it with his good arm. It didn't budge. He tried it with both hands. It was strange, his numb fingers clumsy as he struggled to lift the rock with them, but it worked. He lifted the rock and dropped it to the ground.

"We'll keep using the painmod so we can work," Dritan said.

"We're dead, man. We're never getting out of here. Look at that wall. You think we're going to be able to move all those rocks, with your arm and my fucked up leg?"

"Look—either help or shut up," Dritan said.

McGill leaned against the rock pile, taking the weight off his bad leg. "I bet you're wishing they'd just airlocked you up there with your friends."

Dritan's chest tightened, and he forced himself to take even breaths so he wouldn't waste his oxygen. "And why are you down here? How'd a trained guard end up getting drafted? Didn't they think you were good enough to do the job?"

A nasty smile appeared beneath McGill's mask. "That traitor took my pulse gun. I had nothing to do with him. But you—"

"My *crewmates* were traitors. *I* am *not*."

"No. You're just a snitch. Would the subs even let you live if they knew?"

Dritan stiffened. "I don't know where you got your information. But it's *wrong*."

McGill let out a harsh laugh. "Don't worry. Your secret's safe with me."

Dritan stared down at his blood and grime-covered hands. *I did what I needed to do to protect my family.* He couldn't afford to think about this right now. McGill shouldn't know anything about him. He'd have to deal with this later, once they got out of here. "Just shut up. We need to work."

McGill shook his head, but he hefted a rock from the pile and dropped it to the ground.

Dritan pushed aside thoughts of his crewmates, of what he'd done, and focused on the pile of rock in front of him. Each rock they moved was one step closer to rescue—one step closer to the tube and the promise of the recyc fan beyond.

One step closer to Era.

CHAPTER TEN

Explosives. The word had cycled through Tadeo's mind over and over since he'd seen the empty canister in the terrorists' cubic. Explosives were missing on the *Paragon*, and they could be anywhere.

He strode down the corridor on level six, an archive cube case tucked beneath his arm, high off the threat—the danger of it all. He barely saw the guards who quickly moved out of his path as he plowed by. He passed the guard barracks, the galley, and then hit Central corridor.

His comcuff buzzed.

"Raines."

"Where you at?" came Chief's tense voice.

"Almost there. I have the cubes from the Repository."

"We're in my cubic."

He turned into Central Records. Temporary records were logged here, where colonists had to come to get their shift cards altered for new jobs. Guards sat behind their stationaries, searching through records, doing routine tasks like clearing next week's work schedules.

They looked up as he passed, and a few of them stood.

"Lieutenant Raines," a chorus of voices said.

They stared at him as he went to Chief's work cubic. Omar stood outside it, his hands folded in front of him, a sheen of sweat coating his dark skin.

Tadeo rapped on the door, and it slid open, revealing Chief. Nyssa sat in a chair against the wall.

The president's eyes were bright, intense as she watched him take a seat. The chief picked a bag up from the floor and took out the empty metal canister and placed it on the table before him.

Tadeo read the text engraved on the side, and his heart rate increased.

PARAGON

ARTEX 500
WARNING: HIGHLY EXPLOSIVE

The manufacture date stamped on the canister was only two weeks ago, mere days before the terrorists had been airlocked.

Tadeo laid the archive case on the table beside the canister.

"I'm not calling a board meeting on this yet," Nyssa said, breaking the tense silence. "What is said in this cubic stays in this cubic. Chief? Brief us."

"Artex is only used in mining," Chief said, his voice hard. "The *Perth* makes it, and they've been using it to aid clearing mines on meteors and on Soren. It's tightly regulated. It never should have made it onto the *Paragon*."

"What kind of damage could this amount do?"

"It could damage a few cubics—but the blast would be contained. The damage would be minimal."

They sat in silence for a moment, and Tadeo clenched his hands into fists. He wanted to be out there, searching for it. Not sitting in here.

Nyssa cleared her throat. "I want to know how it got past imports. If the *Moscow* has traitors aboard, they could be smuggling anything anywhere."

The *Moscow* was the fleet's supply deka. Their transports picked up supplies from each deka, then transported them wherever they were needed. The chief had already tried to punish them for turning a blind eye to smugglers and black market thievery, but their board member, Nassef, always seemed to come up empty-handed when it came time to hand over the perpetrators.

Chief pulled some cubes off the shelf behind his table. "I have the terrorists' work orders, as well as the import and export records, but there's no record of any Artex making its way through," he said. "The only time it leaves the *Perth* is when *Moscow* transports bring it to Soren."

"Could it have come from Soren?" Nyssa asked.

"Once it's on Soren, it's just as tightly controlled as it is on the *Perth*. So either someone personally carried it off a transport, or we have traitors on the *Moscow* and definitely in our imports sector. This *had* to have been smuggled over from the *Moscow*."

Nyssa pressed her lips together. "We

need to find the connection between imports and our three terrorists."

Tadeo gestured to the archive case he'd brought. "I ordered work records from the Repository for all recent transfers from the *Perth* and *Moscow*. And I got a list of everyone working in imports and exports, so we can cross-check their work schedules with the terrorists'. But there's a lot to go through. Hundreds of names and dates."

"Thank you, Lieutenant Raines. And Era Corinth? Chief said you found a power cell insert and a medlevel card in her cubic? Have you discovered any connections between the terrorists and what you found?"

Tadeo shifted in his seat and swallowed. "The power cell insert had no ID number—nothing to trace it with. And I don't know where the medlevel card came from yet, but... I do have one lead."

"What is it?" Nyssa asked, leaning forward.

"Tatiana Carizo went to medlevel when she got here. So did Era. And they both saw the same medic. A Nora Faust."

Nyssa darted a glance at Chief but didn't respond. His face was blank, unreadable.

"I think she knows something. She—"

"Clearly just a coincidence," Nyssa said. "All women go to population management annually."

"But—"

"No," Nyssa said, holding up a hand. "If you've made no progress with Era, we need to focus on finding the smugglers."

"Well, I talked to Nora. She acted suspicious, and—"

"Lieutenant Raines," Nyssa said, her voice harsh, "if you haven't found what I told you to search for, the investigation into Era Corinth must be set aside for now. Or would you have us chasing medlevel clerks while we have explosives aboard?"

Tadeo's cheeks warmed. "No, of course not. You're right, Madame President."

"Good. We follow this new lead, then."

Chief cleared his throat and pointed to the archive case. "We have several hundred colonists working in close contact with imports and exports. It's going to take a few shifts to question everyone, even if we narrow it down. We can start with imports."

Tadeo cleared his throat. "Is there anyone else in the sublevels we can—?"

"Any possible traitors are dead,"

Chief said, a smug look on his face.

"I know about the crews who died on Soren, but—"

"Almost all the subs who worked with the terrorists came from the *Meso*. Did you think we'd leave your traitorous kak on our ship? They *all* died in that cave-in. Every last one."

"Enough." Nyssa held up a hand.

Tadeo swallowed. He'd never live down the shame, never be allowed to forget the terrorists came from *his* ship.

"Chief," Nyssa continued. "I want you to assign guards to enforce curfew tonight. No transports will be allowed to board or leave the *Paragon*, but we won't share why. Tomorrow you will question everyone in imports, starting with the *Moscow* and *Perth* transfers."

Chief grunted. "Yes, Madame President."

"Lieutenant Raines," Nyssa said, turning toward him, "come first shift, I want you and your squad investigating the terrorists we airlocked. Look into every site of every single job the terrorist crew worked—from the date this explosive was manufactured to the date they were airlocked." The president stood. "Both of you can take as many squads as you need to get the job done, but keep the details you share to a minimum. We need this to look like we're simply investigating the terrorists' work to ensure nothing else was sabotaged."

"President Sorenson," Tadeo said, "shouldn't we get started searching now?"

Nyssa shook her head. "It's nearly last mess, and if we start now, the board will wonder what's going on. And I don't want them knowing about this. Not yet. You're dismissed."

Tadeo got up to leave, and Chief narrowed his eyes at him as he left the cubic. The door slid closed behind him, leaving the president and Chief alone once more.

Tadeo's heart rate picked back up as he passed the guards in the room. Omar followed him out to the corridor.

"Are we gonna search?" Omar asked, keeping his voice low.

"Tomorrow."

"But—"

"Those are the orders. And we can *not* talk about this again. I'll brief you first shift."

"Yes, sir." Omar rubbed the back of his neck. It was clear he wanted to ask more questions, but he kept his mouth shut.

The last mess buzzer went off, and Tadeo and Omar walked in silence to the command level galley. The meal was tense, and Kiva's attempts at banter with Omar were met with more silence. Tadeo ate quickly and avoided looking at the board members.

As he left the galley, he looked down the main corridor toward the massive doors that led onto the bridge. The terrorists had been from *his* ship. His ship. When he was in charge, he'd make sure nothing like this ever happened again. But how had they managed to slip through the screening process? How had they gotten permission to transfer in the first place? There was so much he didn't know about them. Their records only went back ten months.

Tadeo strode toward the bridge doors. No one except the president, the board, and the captain were authorized to use the private bridge comms, but the president had told him he could comm his mother. And it had been a long time since he'd had a live conversation with her instead of the recorded messages sent through the Comm Station.

He'd ask about Nora Faust and find out what the traitors had been like on the *Meso*. He rested his hand over his pocket and swallowed. Maybe seeing his mother would give him the strength to throw out the grimp.

A guard let Tadeo through the bridge doors, and he stepped onto the gleaming bridge. The glasstex arched across the far end. Black space filled up most of it, and the edge of Soren's red surface filled up the rest. Bits of metal glinted in the distance, glimpses of some of the other ships, as they orbited Soren. The closest ship was the metalworking deka, the *London*.

Paragon's bridge crew worked at their stations, checking data that came in from all over the ship, ensuring that everything ran smoothly. It felt like *home* up here. The bridge was much larger than the *Meso's*, but the low hum and tones, the amazing sight of space... it was everything he'd grown up with.

Except for the captain in the chair. Captain Lopez sat in his seat before a massive clear holo screen that bisected the space. He was aging and gray and only a captain in name. Here, the president and board made the rules. The captain simply did what he was told. When he died, the president would choose a new captain to take his place. There was no family line in charge here. No real lineage to respect. Every deka captain, including Lopez, knew who was really in charge on the *Paragon*. The president.

Lopez sat up in his seat as Tadeo approached him. "Lieutenant Raines? Is something wrong?"

"I need to use the private comm. President's orders."

Lopez activated the eyepiece he wore. "Which ship do you need me to notify?"

"The *Meso*. Captain Lara Raines."

He nodded. "I'll get them on."

Tadeo headed toward the line of doors at the back of the bridge, to the middle one that led to the private comm. He passed through the door and hit the button to shut it behind him. A table and chairs filled the space, and a comm screen took up one wall.

Tadeo picked a chair at the center of the table and sat. The screen flashed in front of him, and the wall faded into a familiar scene: a nearly identical comm cubic on the *Meso*. Except in that cubic, his mother was seated at the table.

Tadeo sat up straight as the connection loaded, but his heart twisted as he took in the sight of his mother. She smiled at him, and he tried to smile back.

He had the same full lips she did, and his own large brown eyes stared back at him. There'd been a running joke on the *Meso* that his mother had such high standards she'd made him in her own image by herself—without his father's help—so she could be sure the ship would be well-run after she died. That's how alike they looked.

But their resemblance had faded. She looked so thin, her high cheekbones sharp, her once tanned skin pasty under the light of the lume bar. And her thick black hair was streaked with gray. Had she looked this old in the messages she'd sent? Why hadn't he noticed? When she'd begged him to visit, he should have gone... no matter how much he dreaded stepping foot back on the ship where he'd lost Kit.

A tone sounded, verifying that the connection was fully established.

"Tadeo," his mother said, smiling.

"Mother."

"It's so good to see you. Does this mean Nyssa talked to you about coming to visit? She says she'll let you take a transport over.

I really need to talk to you. It's important. You're almost twenty-one. I—"

"It's good to see you, but no. This isn't about that."

His mother sat up straight, and her expression turned grim. "What happened?"

Tadeo ran his hand through his hair. Now that he was sitting across from her, he didn't even know where to start. He couldn't tell her everything... why had he even commed her?

"I'm conducting an investigation."

"About..."

"The terrorists. They came from the *Meso*."

His mother glanced away from the holo screen, toward some point near the door. She fiddled with her sleeve. "Yes. They did. The president said they were responsible for the hull breach, but... I'm not convinced. You're lucky you weren't there when it happened."

"Those terrorists *were* responsible."

"Are you certain?"

"We are. And now I need more information on them."

His mother took a deep breath and met his gaze. "I already talked to Nyssa about them. What else do you need to know?"

"How did they get clearance to come here?"

"As I told Nyssa, they were clean. None of them had ever caused any trouble here. There was no indication they would do what they did."

"I need to know what jobs each of them held... What did they do before coming here?"

"What's going on?" Her eyes filled with concern. "They were airlocked. The threat is gone... Isn't it?"

"Just answer my question. What jobs did the terrorists have before they came here?"

"If you want me to help you, you'll tell me."

Tadeo swallowed. "I can't tell you. Nyssa's orders. It's against the rules."

His mother leaned forward. "This is one of those times when you have to know when to break the rules. They exist to protect the colonists of this fleet, but sometimes they get in the way. You should understand that... better than anyone. "

Tadeo's throat thickened, and he held up a hand. "Don't bring that up. That's not why I commed you."

"Isn't it? Isn't it why you haven't visited? Why you won't come home?" His mother asked, her voice low.

"Don't talk about it," Tadeo said, commanding her in the same way he commanded his men.

But she didn't respond to others' commands like his men did. His tone didn't even make her blink. "Maybe we *do* need to talk about it. Isn't it the reason you still haven't found a match? It's your duty—the one thing you must do before you can lead."

Her words stung, and Tadeo tensed. "Has it occurred to you that maybe I don't want to come back because of *you*? Because of your incessant nagging that I pair—your reminders about what happened?"

She jerked back as if he'd slapped her and averted her eyes to focus on her hands. She let the silence go on for a moment. "You've changed," she said quietly.

"Yes," Tadeo said, pushing down discomfort at the hurt look on his mother's face. "I *have* changed. I don't break the rules. I follow them. Now will you answer my questions or not?"

His mother peered at him for a long moment, then settled back in her chair. "If you want my help, you have to tell me everything."

"I can't."

His mother got quiet. "Do you trust me, Tadeo?"

"Of course I trust you."

"You should. Out of everyone on this fleet, I am the one person who will always have your best interests at heart. You know that, don't you? Even if I'm an unfortunate reminder of what happened to you—"

"What I did."

"What *Kit* did to you. She was as responsible as you were—if not more so."

"Stop!"

"If you trust me, and you should, then tell me so I can help you." She leaned closer to the holo screen, searching his face. "Are you in danger? You need to tell me exactly what's going on."

He stared at his mother, his stomach churning. He never should have come here. This was a mistake.

"Do you know a medic named Nora Faust?"

His mother stiffened at the sudden change of topic and then slowly shook her head. Her brow furrowed in confusion. "No. I've never heard that name before. Was she working with them? Please tell me what's happened. I might be able to help."

Tadeo let out a breath. His mother was *not* the enemy, whatever Nora Faust had said about her. And she wasn't a board member, either. The president hadn't told him not to tell his mother. She'd only said she didn't want the board members to know anything. Nyssa had said last night how much she trusted his mother—they were best friends.

Private bridge comm conversations weren't recorded. He *could* tell his mother the truth... no one would know.

"Alright," Tadeo said. "Tatiana, Jonas, and Sam all shared a cubic in singles sector. Today we found an empty canister of Artex explosive powder hidden in the cubic. We have no idea where the powder is."

His mother sucked in a breath, and she stood. She began pacing back and forth before the screen. "Are you *sure* it was their cubic you found the explosives in?"

"Yes."

"I just can't believe... I still don't believe they did it."

"They did. We had all the evidence we needed, and in the end, all three of them confessed."

His mother stopped to wrap one hand around the chair-back, her knuckles white. She closed her eyes for a long moment, and when she opened them, he saw something new there. Resignation.

"I never meant for any of this to happen, Tadeo."

CHAPTER ELEVEN

Tadeo's stomach dropped. "What do you mean—you never meant for this to happen?"

"After four years on the *Paragon*, where do your loyalties lie? Can I trust *you*?"

"Are you serious?" Tadeo's voice rose. "My loyalties lie with you. And with the president and the board. I'm loyal to the fleet."

His mother leaned forward against the chair, her gaze intense. "If I'm going to share information, I need to know I can trust you. What I tell you must not be repeated."

Tadeo's heart sped up. "You want me to keep secrets... from Nyssa?"

"She doesn't know about Kit. No one does. I kept *your* secret. Now I need you to keep mine."

"What did you do?" Tadeo asked, drawing out each word.

His mother paused, then began to pace the room again.

"You asked what jobs the... *traitors* had, and I promise you, none of them had *ever* been in any trouble here. Sam and Jonas had been on maintenance crews since they became halfs. Almost every sublevel worker has spent a cycle on Soren, but other than that, they worked in the sublevels, kept the helios working, repaired hydropods. All of that. But Tatiana... I really trusted her. She was technically a sub, but she reported to me."

Tadeo's chest tightened. "A sub reported to you? Why?"

His mother paused in her pacing and turned to face him. "Tatiana was my eyes and ears."

Tadeo sucked in a breath. The implications of her statement lay like scattered seeds across the table before him. "What are you saying?"

His mother took a seat at the table once more, and her hands were steady, her gaze firm. "Every captain has... agents. Colonists they trust more than others. I would have taught you all of this when you came back here."

"Agents—?"

"You give your agents small favors in exchange for information. They keep an eye on your deka, get a sense if your population is too tightly wound, if the pressure needs to be relieved. You never command alone, Tadeo. Remember that. Quin will succumb to rot if not given a specific blend of nutrients. In the same way, a good leader fails without exactly the right people helping her manage her ship."

Bile rose in Tadeo's throat. "Are telling me that Tatiana was your... your spy? Why did you send her here?"

"She was my *agent*. I sent her there..." His mother gave him a rueful smile and shrugged. "She was supposed to keep an eye on the *Paragon* and send information back."

"You were spying on the president?" Tadeo hissed. He glanced toward the door, and sweat broke out on his forehead. "Did Tatiana happen to tell you she planned to try to *kill* the president and board?"

His mother's expression hardened. "No."

"What did she tell you? How did you communicate? They monitor the comms—"

"She got messages out. But they were... innocuous. They can't be traced to me."

Tadeo swiped a hand through his hair, and the room seemed to tilt off-center. "Have you told the president any of this?"

"Of course not."

"Do you understand what this looks like?"

"I know exactly what it looks like. And that's why you aren't telling anyone. Do you want us to lose our ship? If the board finds out about my connection to Tatiana, that's exactly what will happen. Or worse."

Tadeo rested his head in his hands and stared down at the scratched table, fighting to calm his mind so he could think straight. "Nyssa's your friend. Your closest friend in the fleet. She always has been. You need to tell her. She won't—"

"Our friendship won't matter in this. None of us will hesitate to protect our own interests. You should know that by now. Nyssa protects what's hers. And I protect what's mine."

She didn't need to say that it was *him* she'd protected when he'd needed it the most. Tadeo pulled at his hair, fighting nausea.

PARAGON

His mother pressed her lips together. "I guarantee you that every captain in this fleet has agents aboard the *Paragon*. Nyssa has to know that. She doesn't share everything with me. And the board doesn't tell us anything."

His mother stared at him, her eyes begging him to understand. "They keep us in the dark about their plans for the fleet. And I'm stuck dealing with that asshole board member. Nielsen doesn't give a kak about the *Meso*. Captains need a way to get information, and this is how it's done. It's just the way this game is played—has always been played."

Tadeo slammed his fist on the table. "Except that this is not a fucking game. Your... your spy was involved with terrorists. Terrorists who could have killed *me*. Me and the president and the board. Terrorists who want us all dead and may have planted explosives somewhere on this ship."

His mother blinked a few times and sniffed. "I do what's necessary. And so will you. You'll see. Let's just focus on fixing our current problem."

This was bad. So much worse than he ever could have imagined. And he couldn't tell the president, couldn't let anyone know—*ever*—that Tatiana had been his mother's spy.

"Tell me what jobs Tatiana did for you." His voice came out strong. Commanding.

She gave a single nod of her head, as if approving of his decision to accept her confession and move past it. But he was far from moving past any of this.

"I put Tatiana on special duties," his mother said. "She did maintenance work in sensitive areas. Silo sector, transports, command level, power core, medical..." His mother twisted her hands together. "And other duties. Things she did for me as an agent. I have torn this ship apart since the hull breach. I've had crews go over every inch of every job Tatiana, Jonas, and Sam did. And I've found nothing. Nothing. They were loyal."

His mother looked like she believed every word. But he didn't. He'd seen the records, heard Tatiana's confession. They hadn't even used drugs on her. She'd caved almost immediately. She was a traitor.

And even though he wanted to believe Nyssa would understand, he knew his mother was right. The president would protect her ship at any cost. He'd learned that with Era and McGill. His mother had just put him in a terrible position. He'd have to lie. Hide the truth. *Break the rules.*

"Talk to me," his mother said.

"You know," he said quietly, his voice gruff. "After the hull breach, they sent every *Meso* sublevel worker you transferred here down to Soren. They weren't even there a week when they all died in a cave-in."

His mother put her hand over her chest and took a deep breath. "I'm not responsible..."

Tadeo stood and leaned across the table toward the screen. "Your *game* has gotten a lot of people injured and killed. Now tell me—is there anyone else on this ship that the terrorists may have been working with? Any other *spies* you transferred over here?"

She averted her eyes, waited too long to answer. There *was* someone here still.

"No," she finally said.

"I need to go find the explosives."

"Tadeo—"

He twisted his wrist, and his mother vanished from the screen. Disappointment and anger coursed through him. His memories of her seemed holo now, not real. Maybe she wasn't what he'd built her up to be.

He clenched his jaw and stormed out of the room and through the bridge, feeling curious stares at his back. The corridors leading to his cubic were nearly empty now, with everyone turning in for the night.

His mother. A traitor. He had to tell Nyssa what he'd discovered, didn't he?

But... his mother had protected him when he'd needed it most. She'd lied to keep him safe.

By the time Tadeo reached his cubic, he was breathing hard, and a sheen of sweat coated his face. He tore off his guard suit, and as it fell to the floor, he remembered the grimp.

With a shaking hand, he unzipped the pocket of his suit and pulled out the contents—Era's shift card, taken from Zephyr earlier that day, and the plastic packet of grimp. The blue-green pills beckoned to him, begged him to try just one. He leaned against the wall, staring at them in his hand. They'd erase everything and make this all go away. He could be free of the burden. He wouldn't *care* anymore.

He should send it down the lav. But he didn't. It took everything he had to shove the grimp, and Era's shift card with it, into the depths of his cabinet. Then he fell into his bunk and shut out the lights. He stared up into the darkness, his heart pumping too fast for sleep. His mother sent a spy, a *terrorist*, to this ship. Would Nyssa order her execution if he told the truth?

He slept, but nightmares woke him through the night. Nightmares of his mother—stepping into the control room with him, taking over the controls and airlocking Kit and Era both. But then Nyssa would appear, sentencing his mother to the same fate.

Just before night shift curfew ended, he stole into the empty, half-lit corridors to go to the one place that could bring him comfort and help him clear his mind.

Tadeo's feet pounded the treadmill. The room was dark, his only source of light the holo screen above the machine. His lungs struggled to take in enough oxygen and screamed for him to stop. Every muscle in his legs burned, half-numb, half-tingling, as if he'd jabbed them with needles from a madaro plant. He grimaced against the pain and punched the button, dialing up the speed. In the ship's dented wall panels, his distorted reflection moved faster. A line of rivets ran down the center, splitting his body in two.

My mother is a traitor.

Running hadn't allowed him to escape the truth—it had forced him to admit it.

That was the problem with treadmills. You could never really run anywhere. Not like on the *Meso*, where he'd run the massive levels filled with huge helios and green growing plants. Not the way he'd be able to run on a new Earth if they found it in his lifetime. There'd be open fields and dirt paths like the damaged footage he'd seen of Earth on the few cubes his family possessed. *A better world.* That's what all of this was for, wasn't it?

He ran faster, sweat dripping down his brow, soaking his workout suit. He had to make a decision. Did he tell Nyssa the truth about his mother and hope she'd forgive them? Or should he lie? This should be a simple, easy answer. He was loyal to the president. He should tell her. But the question continued to gnaw at him, until the buzzer rang out, calling an end to night shift. The lume bars in the ceiling flickered to life in the empty gym.

Tadeo's heart pounded against his ribcage, ready to burst.

"Raines."

He misstepped and nearly lost his balance. He jabbed at the interface to shut it down, then hopped off the machine, taking ragged breaths. When he reached for his towel, it was no longer where he'd left it.

Omar stood behind him, already dressed in his navy guard suit. He held out Tadeo's towel. "Dropped this."

Tadeo took it and wiped the sweat from his face.

Omar wrinkled his dark brow and peered at the treadmill. Tadeo's stomach lurched, and he shifted his body between Omar and the machine, so he couldn't see the time count on the holo interface. No one knew Tadeo had an exemption for the curfew, and he'd rather keep it that way.

"How long you been here?" Omar asked.

"Just got here, same as you. What do you think?"

Omar widened his eyes but shrugged. "Where's your commcuff? Chief commed me. He wants us to grab mess and get started. No time for working out. You should get back to him."

Tadeo cleared his throat and wiped his face again. He didn't want to talk to anyone right now. "I'll meet you at mess in a bit."

Omar made a face and twisted the black, bulky comcuff on his own wrist. "You alright, man? You seem..."

Tadeo glanced toward the doors, but they were still alone in the gym. "I have a lot on my mind. Don't you?"

"I do. The canister... How much damage could that kak do?"

"It's enough to take out a few cubics. But we'll find the powder today," Tadeo said.

"Are we gonna tell the whole squad?"

"They'll help us search, but... let me worry about what to say. You don't say anything."

"But shouldn't they know?"

"When it's time, they will. Grab some mess, check out holo gear, and meet me at the conference cubic at Central with the rest of the squad."

Omar's eyes flicked to the treadmill again, but he walked off, leaving Tadeo alone in the empty gym.

He reset the treadmill's holo

screen and headed for the showers, past the long row of weights. The treadmills were the last piece of functioning machinery. White squares stood out on the stained tile where other fitness machines, motors long dead, parts scrapped, had once been bolted down. Two guards entered in their workout suits and halted to salute him.

"Morning, Lieutenant."

"Lieutenant Raines."

Tadeo inclined his head toward them, without making eye contact, and went to shower.

He scoured his tan skin red, dried off, and pulled his suit from his locker. The stiff fabric of his guard suit stuck to his still-damp skin, but he welcomed the unpleasant sensation. It took his mind off the worse feelings roiling in his gut. He leaned against the locker and stared down at spots of rust on the metal floor.

My mother is a traitor.

But I can't betray my family.

There it was. The whole truth he'd been trying to run from. If he had to choose between Nyssa and his mother, he'd choose his mother. She'd been there for him, had broken rules for him.

Hot anger spread within him, and he slammed his fist into the locker. He winced at the pain that shot up his arm. His mother had put him in an impossible position. But when all this was over, he'd pay her a visit. He'd order her to stop her treason, to cease her spying.

And until then, he'd lie for her. He'd find a way to fix this and make it all go away.

CHAPTER TWELVE

Zephyr lay in the darkness of her bunk, privacy panel closed, clutching to her chest the pale green scrap she'd taken from Era's cubic. Once she heard the door slide shut, proof her bunkmates had finally left for first mess, she carefully stored the scrap on the shelf in her bunk, then jumped down and got dressed, fully intending to go to mess. But as she tied on her boots, a sudden wave of panic washed over her. *Screw mess and its half-sized rations.*

She climbed back into bed, her breath coming quickly, and grabbed her handheld and eyepiece from the shelf. She sat there, letting her legs dangle over the edge, and tried to take deep, full breaths.

After sliding on her eyepiece, she gestured to open her music creation program. She'd huddled in her bunk yesterday writing a song. Every hour, she'd heard a voice outside her door that sounded like Era's. When she left to go to the lav, she glimpsed colonists with short brown hair like Era's, and had expected her to show up, to speak in her calming way, say it was all a huge misunderstanding. But it wasn't. Tadeo said they'd seen her body.

Era was dead.

Zephyr wiped her eyes and tapped the sounds she'd chosen, manipulating their arrangement. Swirls of color denoted each instrument, and the program melded them together to create a unique blend of sound.

Music was emotions made manifest. When even her ability to numb herself wasn't enough—when she had nowhere to put the chaotic mess within her—she spilled it into the beat, recycled it into something new. She took a sip of water from her canteen and glanced toward the door again, willing her bunkmates to stay away. Then she gestured to make the program begin recording. She took a deep breath and started to sing. It came out weak at first, but slowly grew in strength as her emotions flowed out of her and into the song.

Wanna stay here with my dreams.
Don't wanna face the day.
'Cause this reality's my nightmare
Since you went away.

Wish I could find faith
In what they call lies
Since the day we lost it all
And the old gods died.

Everywhere,
I see your face.
In every song,
I hear your voice
Like a phantom melody.

Why'd you make that choice?

I wanna believe I'll see you again.
Wanna believe that this isn't the end.
Wanna believe that there's a better world waiting.

Need hope the dead religions give me.

Want a reason, not a chaos theory.
I wanna believe a better world is waiting.

She sang it over and over, until the song held her pain for her, and all that was left was vast *nothingness*.

Being empty always felt better than being full.

Zephyr started up the song again, and the door opened. She glimpsed the corridor, packed tight with halfs.

"She airlocked herself," Kali said.

Kali, Helice, and Paige walked through the door.

Zephyr twisted her wrist angrily, and the holographic display winked out of existence, taking the music with it. She stuffed her eyepiece and handheld in her pocket and zipped it shut.

Paige wrinkled her nose like she'd caught a whiff of compost. "It's a shame you guys have to deal with that hid- eous noise all the time in here."

Zephyr jumped off the bunk. "Yeah, she *is* sick of it. She's just afraid to tell you to shut your face."

Paige colored. "We were just talking about the airlocker. You knew Era, right? So why'd she do it?"

Zephyr met Paige's gaze but didn't answer. The lump in her throat was suddenly back.

Paige turned to her friends. "It's like I told you. Era's husband helped the traitors. That's why they sent him to Soren." She looked back at Zephyr, and a little smile appeared at the corner of her mouth. "We're lucky they're both gone."

Zephyr swallowed and balled her hands into tight fists. "We'd *all* be luckier if you were gone, Paige. In fact, I'm sure I could arrange it."

Paige arched an eyebrow. "You command level kids think everything orbits you. But the truth is..." She paused for effect, then spoke slowly, enunciating each word. "No one wants you here."

Zephyr went rigid with anger, and the other girls exchanged tense looks. Zephyr pressed her arms to her sides, willing herself not to slap the smirk off Paige's face. She wasn't going to get in trouble over this stupid glitch. Paige had been born to techs and never had a shot at being more than a tech. And she wasn't even a *good* tech. Mali had chosen Era, not Paige, to be head archivist, and that had been the best revenge.

Zephyr stalked out of the cubic without a word and took shaky breaths as she weaved her way through the crowded corridor, desperate to get to the stairwell. She still had time before first shift. She'd hide out up in Observation until the last possible moment.

She was breathing hard by the time she reached the observation deck. It was nearly empty at this hour, just a few colonists and children sitting on benches. She made her way to the front and sat down.

Soren filled up most of the view, its swirling red-orange clouds moving across a toxic surface. Deadly beauty. Nothing could survive down there naturally. That planet was as broken and defective as every colonist in this fleet. And if Zephyr's hunch was right, the president might be planning to *stay* there.

Zephyr's gaze moved to the half-circle of metal beside the planet, the jumpgate, and the lump in her throat grew. The gate was a promise—a promise that a better world waited for all of them. But not for Era. Not anymore. She blinked rapidly and tried to calm the wave of grief that threatened to overwhelm her.

Why, Era? Why did you do it?

They'd talked about suicide once before, just before the fleet had reached Soren. An old, sick man on the *London* wasn't able to get a spot in *Paragon*'s hospice, so he airlocked himself. The enforcers there turned a blind eye when one of the elderly chose to end it that way. Some wanted a quick death, not the slow, painful one power core sickness brought.

Era and Zephyr were sitting on Observation when they overheard a paired couple talking about the suicide.

"I knew that man," Era said. "His son works with my father. He shouldn't have shamed his family and friends like that. It was selfish. Cowardly."

Zephyr stared out at the stars and tried to locate the other dekas in the distance. "Well, I think he was brave to do it. If they told me I wouldn't have nonstop drugs for my final miserable days, I'd airlock myself, too."

Era's face darkened, and she squeezed Zephyr's arm, hard. "You better never do that. As long as I'm alive, I demand you stick around."

Zephyr rolled her eyes. "Fine. I'll suffer through it if you suffer through it. Deal?"

Era had smiled. "Deal."

Zephyr's windpipe closed. *Breathe, Zephyr. Calm down.*

I should have been there.

She'd left Era alone when she'd needed her most.

A man in a green maintenance suit crossed in front of Zephyr, carrying a small blond child of three or four. He walked to the glasstex, and Zephyr tensed. *Go away.*

The man crouched before the glass and put the little girl down.

"Bella," he said. "That's where Mama went."

The small child pressed both hands to the glass and then cast a blue-eyed look up at her father. "When's Mama coming back?"

Zephyr's hand went to her chest. Had this man's wife gone down to Soren with Dritan's crew?

The father grabbed the little girl's hand, encompassing it in his own. "Mama..." He broke off and cleared his throat. "This time Mama won't be coming back."

"Why not? She always comes back."

"She went down to the planet to work for our fleet, but there was an accident. And she can't come back."

"But I want to see her now." The little girl's voice rose.

Zephyr started to stand, but the wave of grief threatened to overtake her, and she sank back down on the bench, tears filling her eyes.

"I know you don't understand now," the father said, "but you will. And you still have me."

Bella pulled away and pressed her face to the glass. "I want to go down there and see her."

Her father wrapped a loose arm around her shoulders and turned to look down at the planet, too, his face twisted with grief. A thin woman in a maintenance suit passed before Zephyr's blurring vision to reach them.

"Lanar," she said, "first shift wants the details on the generator repair. Wes called up for you."

Lanar sighed. "I just got off night shift. But I'll be right there. Can you take Bell back to caretaker?"

The woman rested a hand on Lanar's shoulder. "I will."

Lanar lifted his daughter in his arms, and she began to cry and wriggle in his grasp.

"No—I want to stay here."

"Hush," the woman said, hissing the word. "You're much too big to cry."

The little girl's face crumpled, and she buried her face in her father's shoulder to muffle her sputtering cries.

As they walked away, Zephyr wiped at her eyes and trained them on the planet.

She'd swallowed her pride and begged her father for weeks to transfer Era and Dritan to the *Paragon*. In the end, it was probably her mother who had convinced him, just to keep the peace. But what if Zephyr had kept her mouth shut? Would Era and Dritan still be alive now?

She breathed deeply, and it took a few moments to calm herself as she stared out at the planet through a blur of tears. But as the grief faded, something hotter replaced it, something aggressive. A hot flame of anger erupted in her belly.

She clenched her hands into tight fists and let the heat fill her up. Hate for Tadeo and his ugly words, anger at the president for the regulations that had forced Zephyr to leave Era last night. And rage at the planet, at the half-finished jump gate, at the way the fleet and its stupid rules had killed her only friends.

But there was nowhere to put her anger, nowhere to direct it. She tried to numb it, too, but it didn't fade.

Zephyr should have been there, but she hadn't been the one to push Era over the edge. No. It had been the president, sending Dritan to Soren. And the medic, telling Era she had to abort her child. Zephyr wanted them to pay for what they'd done—but how?

First shift buzzer sounded, and Zephyr let out a little scream and jumped off the bench, feeling helpless. Who did you blame when someone ended their own life? You could only blame the person who took it.

But you couldn't punish the dead.

Zephyr made her way up the near-empty stairwell toward the Repository on level four.

She was already late and had thought of skipping shift again, but unlike the grief she'd been drowning in yesterday, only anger flowed through her now—like molten metal. Simmering in her cubic would do her no good.

When she reached the landing, she stopped before the wide metal doors. Era had loved this place *so much*.

Zephyr passed her shift card over the scanner and stepped through the doors. Tall silver archive cabinets ran along the walls beyond the glass panel that bisected the space. All Era had wanted was to care for these archives like the model colonist she'd been.

Heat burned in Zephyr's chest as she passed the busy comm waiting area and headed for the archivist station. They needed the archive files to settle New Earth someday, but the Repository had never held any fascination for her. Her family had the files they needed on the *London* for manufacturing. Every deka had files for their specialization. And that was enough. The Repository had other files, research from Earth, information on settling a new planet. But what use could they be right *now*, especially when only the president and board could access them?

PARAGON

Zephyr stared at the tile floor as she approached the archivist station, and her throat closed up. Two nights ago, Era had curled up right here, right in front of the station, sobbing after finding out Dritan had died. Mali, the head archivist, had helped Zephyr try to soothe her. Maybe she should ask her for a transfer to get away from this place.

Mali stood behind the station working. Her dark-skinned face was blank and her posture rigid. She had cared for Era, too. She might be the only person on this ship who shared Zephyr's grief.

Mali looked up from the station, her eyes swollen and bloodshot. "You're late. And you missed your shift yesterday."

Zephyr handed Mali her shift card. "I'm surprised you're even here."

"The work must still be done. No matter what." Mali got out a handheld and eyepiece and swiped Zephyr's shift card to log the gear into the system.

"Don't you even care?" Zephyr asked, her voice cracking.

Mali didn't look at her. "I have to log data into the archives this shift. I need you—"

"Look at me," Zephyr ordered.

Mali pursed her lips and handed Zephyr the holo gear. "You may be a future deka captain, but here, you're a tech apprentice. Don't speak to me that way again."

"How can you just—"

"Era airlocked herself." Mali shook her head, like that was all the justification she needed for acting like Era wasn't dead.

"And you can just go on... like it didn't even happen—"

"You need to get to work." Mali twisted her wrist to activate her eyepiece. "If you miss another shift, I'm transferring you out of here. There's a waiting list a hundred deep for this place. You're lucky to have a job here. Act like it."

"But Era—"

"I'm done talking about her," Mali snapped. "She shamed herself and abandoned this fleet and her duties. There's nothing else to say about it."

Zephyr tensed her jaw. "I thought you cared about her."

"I did. But a better world awaits." Mali's voice was distant now. Empty. She gestured in the air, working again. "The fleet must move ever onward. As we all must move on.

You're witnessing comms today. Go."

Zephyr tried to ignore the anger ripping a hole in her chest and stalked toward the comm station. *The fleet must move ever onward.*

One day had passed, and the only other person Era had spent time with had already moved on. They would all move on... Everyone would act this way if she tried to talk about Era. She and Era had done it, too, when people talked about suicides. It *was* shameful. How could Era do this?

Zephyr reached the comm station as more colonists entered the Repository, come to record messages for loved ones on other ships. An old tech, Henry, worked the station.

"I'm witnessing messages today," Zephyr said to him. "Where do you want me?"

The man looked at her through aged, watery eyes and gestured to one of the comm cubics. "Cubic eight is fine."

CHAPTER THIRTEEN

Omar and the squad weren't at mess when Tadeo got there, so he grabbed a quick breakfast and headed straight to the conference cubic across from Central Records. They hadn't arrived yet, so he activated his holo gear and began searching through files on the terrorists, gathering a list of every job Sam, Dritan, Jonas, and Tatiana had ever done aboard the ship.

Then he ran a search, looking for anything unusual, any shift card usage that seemed at odds with their work schedule. At first nothing came up. They'd checked in everywhere they were supposed to. But what if they'd been working to cover for each other?

He searched again, this time looking for shift card usage during their shifts.

The results populated, and Tadeo sucked in a breath. There were dozens of instances where each of them were places they shouldn't have been—outside their usual work sectors. It would take hours to analyze and cross-reference everything here with the data he had on the import and export workers.

A knock sounded on the door, and Tadeo went to open it. Omar stood outside with Kiva and the rest of the squad arrayed behind him.

"You ready?" Omar asked.

"Come in here, Sergeant," Tadeo said.

When the door slid shut behind Omar, Tadeo began to pace in front of the table. "I need you to take the squad and at least one maintenance worker—find Gemma from yesterday. Tear apart every repair job the terrorists did. I need to cross-reference data to see if I can find any leads. It would go a lot faster if I had help..."

"I'll stay. Send Kiva and the squad to search," Omar said.

Tadeo stopped pacing. "But can she can be trusted?"

Omar looked offended. "If I say

she's trustworthy, she's trustworthy."

"I wanted an extra person for this mission, but..." Tadeo shook his head.

"You know how many games of chips I played with that girl?" Omar asked. "She's a terrible liar. Loses every time. You can trust her. And when you need her, she always shows up. Plus, Chief approved her. She's good."

Tadeo met Omar's sincere gaze, and for the first time, he felt the chasm that had formed between them. They'd never been that close, but now they were miles apart.

Tadeo had seen death—had caused it. He'd airlocked a traitor secretly in the night and learned a member of the guard had worked with terrorists. His own mother was a traitor. He knew too much now. His naive view of the fleet had been shattered forever, but Omar still believed everything he used to.

"What?" Omar asked. "Why are you looking at me like that?"

"Nothing. I do trust you. More than Kiva. So... I want you to lead the squad on the search. Kiva can stay with me." Tadeo popped the cube out of his handheld. "Here's a list of every job the terrorists did."

Omar took the cube, but he looked unhappy. "Yes, sir."

"Let them all in, Sergeant."

Omar opened the door, and the squad filed in, backs straight, eyes alert and fixed on Tadeo.

He crossed his arms behind his back and stood tall. "Sergeant Omar will be in charge today. You will be tearing apart every job the terrorists performed while on this ship. Practice extreme caution—we believe they may have rigged more than one job to fail." Tadeo made eye contact with Omar and nodded. He opened the door.

"Sergeant Kiva, you're staying with me."

Kiva looked at him, confused, but she stayed put as the rest of the squad filed out.

"Sit down." Tadeo slid the cube case to Kiva from across the table. "Here is a list of every single repair the terrorists made, and every time their shift cards were used starting ten months back when they arrived, up until the day they were airlocked. I want you to collect and sort every instance where one of them was anywhere other than their job sector."

"Yes, sir, but... Sir, can I ask you something?"

"Speak."

"Why are we investigating all of this now? What's going on?" Her voice had an edge of fear to it.

Tadeo folded his arms across his chest, heart rate picking up. "We're merely checking to ensure they did nothing else to sabotage this ship." His voice came out strong, soothing.

Kiva nodded, a look of relief passing over her face.

He'd have to tell her more than that, or she wouldn't be useful to him. But not yet. Because he had something else he needed to do.

"Sir, is there anything I should be looking for in particular?" she asked.

"Just anything out of the ordinary. I need to get more information from the archives. Start sorting the data by name, date, and sector, and I'll be back soon."

"Yes, sir." Kiva activated her eyepiece. She opened up the metal box, revealing dozens of small data cubes, picked one up, and slid it into her handheld.

Tadeo headed out the door, his heart pumping hard in his chest. A spike of adrenaline surged through him as he strode toward the stairs. The data on those cubes couldn't answer the questions he really needed answers to.

Maybe the most recent *Meso* transfers were dead or had been cleared—but his mother had acted guilty when he'd confronted her.

Someone else was spying for her... and could have been working with Tatiana. He needed information from the archives. He had to break the rules—and lie—if he wanted to find answers.

Tadeo's pulse raced as he passed through the sliding doors of the Repository. Sweat dripped down his back, and his suit stuck to him as if he'd just come from the sublevels.

The large room opened before him, reminding him of one of the helio sectors on the *Meso*. But this space was lit with lume bars instead of a superhelio, and it ended too soon at the glasstex barrier that ran from one wall to the other.

Beyond the barrier, the archive boxes marched along in straight rows, extending back to the dim reaches of the level.

Tadeo strode past the comm station. It was busy in here, the benches packed full with colonists waiting to record messages. The low murmur of the waiting crowd quieted as he passed. Tadeo headed for the archivist station and kept his eyes straight ahead on the archives beyond the barrier.

The memory cubes in each box stored the data they'd need once they found New Earth. They'd relearn ancient farming techniques, restart entire manufacturing chains. Only they'd do it the right way this time. This time, the planet would not be destroyed. There'd be no gen-modded plants, no gen-modded bacteria. Humanity would finally get the chance to start over.

A little twinge of regret ached in him. This place had always represented something pure—the hope of a better world. But now it seemed different, touched by rot after his mother's confession, altered by what Era did. His chest flared hotter than a helio at the thought of Era deleting files, destroying their future, and he quickened his pace. Messing with the archives carried a high price, and she'd paid it.

When all this was over, he'd make his mother see who the real enemy was. And it wasn't the fleet's government. Yet here he was—about to break government rules because of her. Every archive cube order came from the president. And he had to convince the head archivist to pull records he had no official order for.

She stood behind the counter and her large black stationary box, her eyepiece activated, rubbing the smooth dark skin of her forehead. She'd been crying yesterday when Tadeo came in for the import and export personnel files, but now she looked composed. Her bloodshot eyes flicked toward him, and she folded her hands in front of her. "Lieutenant Raines, what can I do for you?"

Tadeo licked his lips and slid his shift card across the counter. "Personnel records."

Mali waited a moment, then her brow furrowed. "Where's the order cube?"

"No cube."

"I need—"

"It's a verbal order."

Mali raised a brow. "A verbal order from the president?"

Another surge of adrenaline flowed

through Tadeo. "Are you questioning my orders?"

Mali bit her lip and backed up from him a small step. She glanced toward the comm station. "I... I can't pull archival records without an official order."

"I'm on the president's *personal* guard now, Archivist. And we need this order now."

"I have to have an order cube," she said, wringing her hands together. "That's the rule."

Tadeo leaned over the counter and met her gaze. She looked *frightened* of him. *Good.*

"This is an urgent records pull for an ongoing investigation," Tadeo said, warning in his voice. "And you *will* pull it now."

"The cube order—"

"Pull it now," Tadeo commanded.

"I can't do it," Mali said. She swallowed hard and pushed his shift card back to him.

"Can't or won't?" Tadeo's pulse buzzed in his ears, and a tiny edge of discomfort spread within him at the thought that he might not be successful in this.

Mali blinked and pressed her lips together.

He placed his hand over his card, making to take it back. "You'll be punished for disobeying a direct order from the president's personal guard," he said, his voice smooth. "I hope you have someone ready to take your place."

Mali set her jaw and didn't respond. His mouth went dry. He needed to try harder. He wasn't leaving empty-handed, not after taking this risk.

"We're investigating Era Corinth's death," he said, keeping his voice low. "I shouldn't tell you that, but you ought to know which investigation you're blocking."

Mali's face crumpled for a moment, and she grabbed Tadeo's sleeve, clearly fighting to compose herself.

He waited, watching her face, and another drop of sweat trickled down his back. He fought to repress a smile. He was enjoying this too much—the *wrongness* of it, the threat of being caught—yet he was using this woman's grief to attain his own ends. He pushed the thought away. Mali had clearly cared about the girl, but she wouldn't if she knew the truth.

Mali finally nodded and glanced toward the front of the Repository again, at the comm station. She released her grip on his sleeve and took his shift card back to scan it. "Tell me what you need."

Tadeo kept his face blank, but his

chest lightened with his success. "Records on every *Meso* transfer who still lives aboard the *Paragon*. And recent records on the colonists who died while on term here."

Mali twisted her wrist to activate her eyepiece and moved her hand in a flurry of gestures, manipulating the 3D interface. "Those records go back three terms—fifteen years. Everyone who came over four terms ago is either deceased or transferred to other ships. Is there anything else?"

"Yes. I want each of their work records for the past ten months. All of them. Every job they did, every time they used their shift card."

Mali hesitated and looked like she wanted to ask him something. She licked her lips and met his gaze. "When do you need this by?"

"As soon as possible."

"I'll get on it now." She handed back his shift card, and Tadeo waited. He wiped the thin layer of sweat from his brow and pressed his hand to the cool, metal counter. His lies had worked, but now his card would be logged as ordering these records. The president had said he had *all* resources at his disposal, hadn't she? If she found out about this, he'd say he thought this was what she meant. Besides, these were just old personnel files. It wasn't like he was accessing ancient Earth files.

Mali finished what she was doing and headed for the storage cubic to retrieve an archive cube case. Tadeo watched her go. If Era had been working with terrorists, she hadn't hidden data in her own cubic. He still didn't know how she might be connected to this, but if Omar's search turned up nothing, he'd convince the president to let them bring squads in here to tear the panels off every last cubic Era had access to.

The repository doors slid open, and a group of talkative halfs walked through and sat at the comm station benches. A girl with brown hair gave him a wave and a bright grin. She looked familiar... was she one of the techs who worked second shift? Tadeo averted his eyes. He had no idea what her name was, and he didn't care. Just another annoyance he didn't need.

He paced to the back of the Repository, out of view of the comm station benches, and leaned against the glasstex barrier. He separated his collar from his damp neck and watched as Mali entered the archives, cube case in hand. If his mother had been up to anything more than what she'd confessed to—he'd know soon.

His comcuff buzzed, and he jolted. Central was comming.

"Lieutenant Raines here," he said, his mouth dry, his eyes glued to the archives.

"Sir, medlevel is on the line. Do you want us to patch them through?"

"Yes." They must have news about the medlevel card he'd found in Dritan's cubic.

The tech from medlevel came on the line. "Sorry for the wait, sir. The card's ancient. More than 30 years. It's not even attached to anyone in our system. I don't know how it's even still around."

Tadeo sighed. "Understood."

He shut off his comcuff. So the power cell insert he'd found in Dritan's cubic was recyc junk, and the medlevel card was a dead end. Only Dritan and Era could tell him why those things had been hidden there, and they were both gone.

Mali exited the archives, and his heart thumped harder at the sight of the case in her hands.

She walked over and handed it to him. "Here's everything."

Tadeo took the cube box in one slick palm. "I need a private space. A cubic."

Mali's brow furrowed, but she nodded and led him toward the side of the Repository. She opened a small cubic with a table and two chairs inside. "Does this work for you, sir?"

"Yes. You're dismissed."

Tadeo dropped into a chair as the door closed behind him. He opened the silver case to retrieve the palm-sized cube within it. A thrill raced through him as he pushed it into the slot in his handheld and activated his eyepiece.

Tadeo gestured impatiently to get past the loading screen, and the main screen appeared, square files dotting it. He tapped the one labeled *Meso Transfer Lists*.

They were listed by date, then sorted by job and last name. He flicked his finger through the air, moving the files as he went through them.

Like Chief had said, every single sublevel worker from the latest transfer list had the same label: *Deceased*.

He paused when he came to Tatiana Carizo's file. The girl had been a year younger than him and looked posi- tively ordinary. Medium-brown skin, straight black hair pulled tight into a ponytail. She wore a blank expression in her holo image.

What were you up to?

He moved past her image and kept going. A dozen other *Meso* transfers had come in during the last transfer term. They worked in the galley as techs, and one worked on medlevel. *Caden Bjork.* The man looked to be near fifty, with pale-hair and light eyes. He saved Caden for later, so he could check to see if the man worked closely with Medic Faust.

He closed out the file and chose the next list of names. This list was much shorter...not many colonists managed to stay on the *Paragon* for longer than one five-year term. Every sublevel worker from ten years back was also marked deceased. The rest worked in the galley, bridge, and helio sector... *imports.* Tadeo tapped *Imports,* and one name came up. *Jai Florian.*

Jai had brown skin, deep wrinkles on his brow, and wore his hair cropped close to his skull. Tadeo tapped his records. The man had no marks against him, had never even been thrown in the brig. His record was impeccable.

But his mother needed someone on the inside capable of smuggling out information. And the *Meso* transfers had known someone with access to the imports and exports sector on zero deck. This man had that access.

He also could have helped smuggle the explosive powder in.

He was the one. Jai Florian was the man he needed to talk to next.

Tadeo hurriedly searched fifteen years back, expecting no useful results. The list only contained one job sector.

Medlevel.

He tapped it, and one image appeared.

Nora Faust.

He swallowed, and his heart thumped unevenly as he opened her records.

Medic Faust had lied. She hadn't been on the *Paragon* her whole life. She'd come from the *Meso*. And Tadeo had no doubt she knew his mother. But was she also a spy? And why would she say the things she'd said if she was?

Jai Florian and Nora Faust.

Had either of them been working with Tatiana?

If either of them had, he was going to make them tell him every- thing... no matter

PARAGON

what it took.

CHAPTER FOURTEEN

Zephyr activated the vidrelay and sat back in her seat. This job was mind-numbingly boring—not interesting enough to keep her thoughts from going to the worst place they could. *Era.*

"Go ahead," Zephyr said, waving a hand.

The young half in the chair across from her shifted uncomfortably. "Name: Brianne Cho, Message for: Kim Cho, of the *Vancouver*."

The girl began to talk, and Zephyr tuned her out. In the past hour, she'd figured out what needed to be done. She had to go to the president and plea for her release.

At age 12, Zephyr became a half, but it was mandated that she spend most of her half years—from age sixteen until twenty-one—

aboard the *Paragon,* so she could learn how the rest of the colonists lived and get to know the president and board. They'd only allow her go home when she turned twenty-one, or if her father died, whichever came first. She'd been secretly hoping her father *would* die before she went back to the *London,* but staying here now, without Era, would be worse than living under the threat of his temper.

She stared hard at the door behind the half, tracing its scratches and dents with her eyes, trying to keep her senseless anger at bay. If she leaned to the right and looked around the half, she could see that the door had a peculiar zig-zag scratch running down the side of it, with a spiral imprint just above it, as if some sublevel worker had hit it with the wrong hot tool. *Someone like Dritan.*

She just wanted to get back to her bunk and sleep or go to Observation to work on her song. Get away from this place.

The half finished talking, and Zephyr grabbed the cube from her handheld and led the girl into the waiting area.

The crowd had grown enormously since she'd started shift, which was strange considering comms wouldn't even be going out for over a week.

"Tadeo," a voice said.

Zephyr stopped walking to turn toward the voice she'd heard.

Paige, Helice, and Kali were sitting on one of the benches, staring toward the archivist station. Zephyr followed their gazes, and her heart sped up. Tadeo stood beside the glass barrier, looking into the archives. Her hate for him flared up, and her cheeks flushed as it ran through her. She'd never speak to *him* again— not after the way he'd talked about Era yesterday.

"Yeah," Paige said. "He came in for a cube order yesterday. He looked *really* happy to see me. I'm sure we'll match up soon."

Helice leaned toward Paige, her dull-brown hair hanging in her pinched face. "And if he wants to pair with you... would you go to the *Meso*?"

Paige batted her lashes and smiled. "Who knows? I have so much to consider now. I'm not sure I can leave here."

"But didn't Kali say that a girl on the *Meso* disappeared because of Tadeo?" Helice asked in a hushed tone. "And that they never found her body?"

"That's only one of the rumors," Kali said, a smug look on her face. "But even if it isn't true, I still wouldn't bother. Everyone knows he doesn't like *women*. I heard he likes—"

"Ugh! Stop talking," Paige said. "It's just a rumor. When he asks me to match, I'm saying yes. Then I'll find out for myself. And maybe, if you're lucky, I'll tell you guys what it's like to match up with the heir to the *Meso*."

Sudden irritation surged through Zephyr, and she laughed, loudly. She hated Tadeo, but she hated Paige more. All three girls turned around, finally seeing her.

"I can't imagine why you'd think he'd want to match with *you*," Zephyr said hotly. "I mean... Tadeo and I have been matching up for a while now. You're *so* not his type."

Paige's face twisted into a jealous pout, and Zephyr smirked as she headed for the outgoing message table. Getting to Paige ought make her feel better—but it only made her feel worse.

"This one goes to the *Vancouver*," she said, handing the comm cube to Henry. "What's going on with this crowd?"

"People have asked if we're shutting down comms." Henry dropped the cube in with the other outgoing messages. "But Mali would have told me if we were. We're not. Everyone coming in is saying it."

Zephyr sighed and glanced longingly toward the doors. "Who's next?"

Henry gestured to check the list on his handheld. "Paige Narula," he called out.

Zephyr bit back a laugh. Of course. That would be her luck. "Can I take the next person instead?"

"If you have issues with her, work them out." Henry pointed in the direction of the crowd. "I don't have enough techs as it is. You're taking her."

Zephyr grabbed a blank cube and turned, bumping right into Paige. "I'm your witness," Zephyr said.

She pushed past Paige and led the way back to cubic eight. Maybe she'd delete whatever Paige recorded and pretend it was a glitch. A glitch for the biggest glitch on the ship.

They entered the recording cubic, and Zephyr pushed the new cube into her handheld and sat down, folding her hands before her.

Paige sat across from her, an ugly expression on her face. "You're such a liar. But you're a *Kerrigan*, so I guess I should expect that."

"Wow. Insulting a future captain. You sure you've got enough brain cells to be a tech?"

"Tadeo would never match with *you*."

"Well, since you're so close to Tadeo now, why don't you just ask him yourself?"

Paige blinked her large blue eyes and sniffed. "I'd like to record my message now."

Zephyr activated the vidrelay and leaned back in her chair.

Paige sat up straight, and her entire face changed, shifting from bitter to bright in an instant. "Name: Paige Narula. Message for: Gerry Monahan, of the *Dubai*. Hey Gerry, I got your last message," she said, her voice cheery. "I'm glad things are going well. I'm *sure* you heard what happened here with our hull."

Paige was skirting around the edge of what was allowed in a comm, mentioning the hull breach like that. Too bad it wasn't enough for Zephyr to report her. She'd have to give specifics, and she obviously knew better than to do that.

"I have such great news," Paige continued, "Mali told me yester- day I've been chosen to be the next head archivist!"

Zephyr grunted in pain, as if Mali had just come into the cubic and kicked her. Had she really moved on *that* quickly? She couldn't even wait one day after Era died to find her replacement? Paige darted a glance at Zephyr and seemed pleased by the expression on her face.

"There was another girl in the running for head archivist," Paige said. "Unfortunately, the job was too much for her. She was an airlocker," Paige said, with a heavy air of judgment. "It's the talk of the ship. But I'm sure she had other reasons for wanting to end it. She was *all* alone. No real friends."

Zephyr pressed her arms to the table, and her vision tinted red. This glitch was *asking* to be punched right now.

Paige smiled again into the vidrelay. "I'll be busy training, so don't be surprised if you don't hear from me for a while. I hope you're trying to get another term over here. Once I'm head archivist, I'll make *sure* they approve your transfer. When you come back, you'll be working with me again. And I know exactly how I'm going to clear out a spot for you." Paige's gaze flicked to Zephyr, then back to the vidrelay.

"*You* won't be stuck on the waiting list. Talk to you soon!"

Paige jumped up from her seat, and Zephyr turned off the relay. Heat coursed through every limb of her body, and lights seemed to dance before her eyes. She gripped the handheld tightly to stop herself from throwing it at Paige.

"You better go drop that in outgoing." Paige's eyes glinted nastily in the light of the lume bar. "I'm working the case second shift, so I'll know if you don't put it in there. Unless, of course, Mali's ready to start training me today."

Zephyr kept her lips pressed tightly together as Paige walked out. Then she tore off her eyepiece and dropped it to the table. It wasn't fair. How could the fleet lose someone as sweet and loyal as Era, yet the colonist who least deserved to live got rewarded?

She ripped her personal holo gear from where she'd hidden it in her suit. She always carried it with her everywhere, so glitches like Paige couldn't steal it from her bunk.

It was against the rules to have outside tech in the Repository, but the rule was stupid, and Zephyr had made it a policy a long time ago to only follow rules she agreed with. If only she'd had the foresight to disobey the curfew regulation, too.

She set up her handheld and pushed Paige's message cube into the slot. Her breath came in quick gasps, and she tried to slow it down as she put on her own eyepiece and opened up Paige's message on her handheld. No one would be able to prove she accessed it, because her handheld and eyepiece were unregistered, untraceable.

She watched the message again, slicing angrily through the air with her finger, deleting chunks of speech and moving others. With grim satisfaction, she moved the segments around until the thick feeling in her windpipe vanished and she could breathe again. After a few minutes of work, she played Paige's *new* message.

"Hey, Gerry, I got your last message," Paige said. "I'm *all* alone. I have no real friends. I *sure* hope you're trying to get another term over here. You'll be stuck working with me again. I'm going to be waiting for you! If you don't come back to me, I'll be an airlocker."

She took out Paige's message cube and shoved her handheld and eyepiece back into her suit. So what if it was immature? Maybe she *was* giving in to caretaker sector mentality, but Paige deserved worse. Far, far worse.

As Zephyr brought Paige's new message to Henry, she felt Helice, Paige, and Kali all staring at her. She glanced across the room as she walked, and her pulse quickened. Tadeo was exiting a cubic on the other side of the Repository.

Who cares, Zephyr? You hate him. And he deserves to be hated.

Zephyr dropped Paige's message into Henry's hand. "*Dubai*," she said.

Paige walked by her at that moment and sidestepped, shoving Zephyr into the table.

"Oops. Sorry," Paige said quietly, too low for anyone but Zephyr to hear. "I've got to go talk to Tadeo. If he's matching up with you, he must be desperate." She started to walk away.

Rage bolted through Zephyr, and she shoved Paige hard in the back. Paige stumbled and whirled around, a shocked look on her face.

"Don't touch me again," Zephyr said in a low growl.

Paige's shock faded, and her eyes crinkled in amusement. "You know, at least Era could take a hint," she said, keeping her voice low. "Go airlock yourself."

Zephyr let out a guttural scream and lunged at Paige, tackling her to the hard tiles. Paige tried to twist away, but Zephyr had her pinned to the floor.

She swung at Paige's face, and as her fist connected with bone, something cracked beneath her knuckles. Blood gushed from Paige's nose, but Zephyr kept going, pummeling her face, her nose, her cheeks, slamming her head into the tiles again and again. Paige took a few weak swings back, but Zephyr blocked them all.

Shouts rose around them, and Paige managed to wrap a hand around Zephyr's long hair. She pulled, ripping a chunk out, but Zephyr didn't even feel the pain. She squeezed Paige's arm until Paige gasped in pain, and her fist relented, opening to let the clump of red-blonde hair drift to the floor. Zephyr tore a chunk of hair from Paige's head in retribution, then punched her again.

Blood spread across her knuckles, and she didn't know and didn't care if any of it was her own. There was only black rage and nothing else.

Paige's face was obscured by slick red when someone grabbed Zephyr from behind and dragged her to her feet. She tried to push the person off as Paige escaped, sliding her broken body across the red-splattered tiles.

"Let me go," Zephyr yelled, flailing her arms, kicking her legs in Paige's direction. Then she saw the navy cloth, the silver infinity symbols printed on the sleeves of the man who held her.

He pinned her arms against her body so tightly she cried out.

"Stop it, Zephyr."

Dubai me. If you hadn't pulled her off of me... I don't know what she would've done to me."

Mali lifted a handheld and an eyepiece off the floor. The casing was crushed, and a crack ran through it, so a bundle of exposed wires hung out. Zephyr gasped.

"Who checked this gear out?" Mali asked. "This isn't one of ours. It shouldn't be in here."

"It's mine," Zephyr said, her voice shaking. "Give those back."

Mali frowned and handed Tadeo the broken handheld and eyepiece. "I assume Zephyr will be spending plenty of time in the brig?"

Tadeo ground his teeth and pocketed the evidence. Then he turned back to Zephyr. "Why did you attack her?"

"She said..." Zephyr pressed her lips together and tried to move her arms, but the cuffs kept them locked behind her back. "Does it really matter what she said? Just let me go. I won't punch her again. Even if she *does* deserve it."

Tadeo scanned the crowd and stopped at the halfs who had stayed nearby. Tadeo focused on a frightened, narrow-faced girl. "What's your name?"

"My name's Helice." The name came out in a whisper.

"What happened here?"

Helice looked at Paige, and her shoulders sunk lower. "Zephyr attacked Paige. Paige didn't do anything."

Murmurs of agreement came from the benches, and the blonde beside Helice nodded vigorously.

Tadeo sighed and turned back to Zephyr. She set her jaw and stared at the broken handheld in his grasp, her expression hard, her eyes like pale blue sparks. When was the last time he'd thrown a girl in the brig? His eyes ran down Zephyr's body. She looked so... feminine. Delicate, not at all like she could deliver the kind of damage Paige's face had taken.

Enough of this. He was wasting precious time. Tadeo blew out a breath. "Okay. Medic, get Paige up to medlevel to get checked. Zephyr's heading to the brig."

Paige gave Tadeo another grateful smile, and Tadeo gave her a slight nod. He grabbed Zephyr harshly, his muscles tense, and steered her out the doors and into the stairwell.

As a future captain, she was an embarrassment to the fleet, tearing up a tech's face like this—in public, no less. Zephyr arched her neck to try to look at him. "I can walk to the brig myself. You don't have to push."

Tadeo kept his hand on her back and guided her up the near-empty stairwell. "You're a future captain."

"So are you."

"Well, act like one," Tadeo said gruffly. "You're supposed to set a good example."

"You think you set a good example?"

"I'm a *Paragon* guard."

"Oh, right," Zephyr let out a broken laugh. "Well, at least the deka captains don't need pulseguns to keep their colonists in line."

"Oh—they don't? This fleet would be safer if there were guards like me on every ship."

"The deka captains have their Enforcers. They don't *want* you on their ships."

"The *Kyoto* wanted us."

"The *Kyoto* captain couldn't exactly give his permission."

Tadeo ground his teeth. "Because rioters *airlocked* him. See? You just proved my point. The ships need us. There has not been a single event on the *Kyoto* since we sent guards over there. A good leader keeps his colonists in line."

Zephyr raised her brows. "Okay, wise leader. Train me. Which leadership method works better for you? Pointing your pulsegun at colonists or threatening to airlock them?"

Tadeo felt the color drain from his face, and his throat thickened. He took a moment before responding. "Either one works," he said, tightening his hold on Zephyr's arms. "Of course, you could always just *beat* all the colonists who don't agree with you."

Zephyr went rigid and pulled away to try to face him. "Is it true what they say about you? That you made a girl disappear on the *Meso*?

Or were you just such a horrible person that she did whatever she could to get away from you?"

Nausea hit Tadeo full force. He took a few quick breaths, balling his hands into fists, and met her angry gaze. "Careful, Zephyr. You don't know *anything*."

"And you don't know me." She stared him down. "And to think we were matching up. Thanks for showing me who you *really* are. Guess I dodged a meteor on that one."

He held her gaze, his jaw clenched tight, but all he could think of was Era. Zephyr's friend. A traitor. Pregnant and naked in the airlock. Tadeo broke eye contact first. "Walk."

Zephyr tossed her head and kept walking up the stairs, her hips moving back and forth, her head held high. Heat flared within him again.

Woe to the *London*. They were screwed if Zephyr was to be their future captain. He'd made a mistake ever saying he'd match up with her. During the few hours they'd spent together, she'd been polite, boring even, her personality as plain as unsalted quin. Obviously she'd been hiding her true nature. This girl was trouble. And he did not have time for more trouble right now.

Squads of guards clogged the corridors of level six, standing in front of the holo screens on the wall, seeking their patrol schedule for second shift. They moved out of the way when they caught sight of Tadeo and Zephyr heading to the brig.

The brig was the size of the command galley but looked like something that had been thrown together after the ship had been built. Like they'd knocked down the walls of a few storage cubics to cobble together holding cells. The bars didn't even open with a shift card—they had locks and took an old-fashioned metal key. It was as if Infinitek—the corporation that had built this fleet—hadn't planned on *needing* a brig.

Since the treason talkers they'd arrested had gone out on the transport early yesterday, the cells were empty, except for the one on the end. Nora Faust lay on the bunk sleeping.

Officer Holt, the gangly, orange-haired brig guard, looked up from his metal counter. "Lieutenant Raines."

"Holt, I need to book this one. And I need you to release the medic to me."

Holt's face paled. "The medic just took a sedative."

"*What?*" he snapped. "Who told you to give her that?"

"I... I'm sorry Lieutenant. Medics came up with her hourly dose. I thought—"

"Don't allow it again. Understand?"

"Yes, sir," Holt said, swallowing.

Tadeo shoved Zephyr toward the high counter. "This one assaulted another colonist. She gets the twenty-four hour minimum. Unless I decide she needs some more time in holding."

"Information, sir?" Holt asked, activating his eyepiece.

"Zephyr Kerrigan, of the *London*," Tadeo said. "Repository apprentice tech."

Zephyr narrowed her eyes at Tadeo. "Repository apprentice tech. And future *captain* of the *London*," she said, biting off each word.

Holt's brows lifted, but he kept gesturing, logging her information.

Tadeo rolled his shoulders, his suit suddenly feeling too tight. Much like the suit Zephyr was wearing. It was like someone over on the *Vancouver* had her exact measurements and had manufactured it to hug her everywhere. Tadeo adjusted the sleeves of his suit as Holt moved around the counter and opened the cell next to Nora Faust's.

"Give me my handheld," Zephyr said.

"Can't have it in there."

"Give it to me. It's mine."

Tadeo ran a hand through his hair, pushing it out of his eyes. "You can apply to get it back from evidence in a few days. Then *maybe* I'll release it to you."

Tadeo removed Zephyr's cuffs, and she shook him off and stalked into the cell. She sank down on the bunk inside and continued to glare at him as Holt closed the barred door.

"This goes to evidence," Tadeo said, handing Holt the holo gear.

"Yes, sir."

"Comm me the minute the other prisoner wakes up."

"Yes, sir."

Tadeo felt Zephyr's eyes boring into him, but he didn't look at her again.

His comcuff buzzed. Omar was calling. He answered as he exited the brig.

"We found more," Omar's voice came through Tadeo's earbud—and he sounded afraid, breathless.

Tadeo froze. "More of what?"

"More empty containers of explosives—behind a wall panel in paired sector."

"I'll comm Chief."

"Wait—there's something else. One of the canisters says Zenith."

"Zenith—"

"Finnegan here's from the *Perth*, and he says Zenith is used to intensify explosions..." Omar paused. "The terrorists had at least five canisters of Artex powder. Zenith could make an explosion a hundred times stronger."

CHAPTER SIXTEEN

Darkness and dirt. Sweat and pain.

The metallic-taste of the oxygen pack reminded Dritan with every breath that he was living on borrowed time. The rock pile seemed to waver before him, as if he stood in the center of a blistering hot power core. They'd barely made a dent in it—if they'd come any closer to the exit, he couldn't tell. His painmod was wearing off, and they only had four shots and twelve hours of oxygen left. That was it.

My life is numbered in hours.

A sharp burst of fear turned his saliva bitter, and he swallowed it back. He'd been in tough spots before. When you looked into the face of death, you had to keep your kak together. *A clear mind and determination keep men alive.* That's what his first crew leader had taught him. And Dritan had seen men survive terrible accidents before. But he'd seen more of them die.

Dritan wedged his fingers beneath another rock and pulled. Darkness swam across his vision as he dropped the stone to the ground. Pain raced up his arm and left him gasping. The shock of it was worse than any cut he'd endured, worse than any of the times he'd been burned on the *London*. The sharp ache radiated from his fingertips to his chest, screaming at him to stop moving.

Then the world disappeared. When he opened his eyes, he was flat on his back, panting, pain raging through him.

"Corinth." McGill was standing over to him, medkit in hand. "Here." He took out a shot and plunged it into Dritan's arm.

The pain faded until Dritan could breathe again. He was messing up his arm, and it might never be right again. But he couldn't stop. If he had to choose between his arm and his life with Era, he'd choose life—even if that meant becoming a sublevel outcast, scorned like the other maimed Soren survivors.

He stumbled to his feet. "I'm going to check on Jan. She's probably almost out of oxygen."

"And what? You gonna give her one of ours?" McGill lifted the canteen to take a sip, and when he remembered it was dry, he threw the empty container down in disgust. "Does she have water, too? I say if she has anything left, you take it. You've wasted enough on her."

Anger stirred in Dritan, surfaced above his exhaustion. He'd checked on Jan once already since he'd found McGill, and she'd been hanging on just fine.

"You think your life is worth more than hers?" Dritan asked, his voice rough. "Must be your exec sector mindset. Say it again, and I'll be giving your packs to her. I'd save her before I'd save you."

Dritan walked off with the last charged helio, leaving McGill to fumble in the dark for a glow bar.

"You know I'm right," McGill called out as Dritan reached the crevice.

Dritan deactivated the helio and pushed his body into the space between the rocks. He began inching forward, back toward Jan. McGill wasn't right. As long as he and McGill kept working, they *all* had a chance of surviving this.

Bad water dripped somewhere in the crevice, and his dry mouth ached in response. *So thirsty.* The cold walls pressed against him, sharp edges jutting into his skin. He made it through quickly, and then he was out to the other side.

"Jan, you still okay?"

No answer.

"Jan?" Dritan tapped the helio, and it floated beside him as he made his way toward her. When the light of his helio reached her, his throat closed up, and his legs weakened.

Jan's eyes were closed, like she was sleeping, but the color of her skin didn't look right. He hurried to her side and knelt to shake her.

"Jan. Wake up." She didn't stir, and her body felt ice cold beneath his fingertips. "Come on. You can make it through. We're making progress..."

He shook her again, and her body slumped to the side. Dritan squeezed her oxygen pack. Still some left. She was *not* dead. He'd promised he'd get her out of here. Panic rose in him as he shook her again. Her body listed further to the side, and she didn't respond.

"No, no, no." His eyes burned, and he glanced toward her leg, at the puddle of blood beneath it. It had gelled, nearly dried up. She'd stopped bleeding a while ago.

"Jan!" He shook her again and held his ear to her chest. She felt colder than the rock. *Stiff.* He choked down a sob and sat back on his heels.

No breath. No pulse.

She was dead, and there would be no bringing her back.

Dritan propped her gently into sitting position and sank down beside her. His helio cast a yellow glow over her as he removed her mask and dropped it into his lap. Her skin was a mottled—blue-gray. She looked almost peaceful, like she'd died in her sleep.

Pain swelled in Dritan's throat. He should have known right away she was dead. She'd died alone. He should have stayed with her.

"I'm sorry," he whispered.

He rested his head against the wall beside her, and everything seemed to close in on him, suffocate him. His breathing came quicker, and he checked his oxygen pack. Still full.

It's all in your head. Calm the fuck down.

He wasn't suffocating. These walls were not caving in. At least not right now.

He closed his eyes and took a deep breath. Jan had been right. It wasn't fair. It wasn't fair that she'd died down here—and for what? Nothing. She'd died for nothing, and he hadn't been able to save her.

She'd been the only member of his crew to be kind to Era... even to Zephyr. She hadn't held their exec level status against them as he knew his other crewmates had. She was one of the good ones. But death didn't care how good you were.

Dritan pounded a fist into the dirt and let out a growl of frustration. He pulled down the zipper of Jan's suit, eyes burning, and removed the necklace she'd shown him, his fingers brushing her freezing skin.

He held the necklace up to the light. It was a battered infinity symbol, taken from a broken machine. It must have come from metal recyc. He slid the necklace into his pocket and zipped it shut.

"I'm sorry," he said again. "I promised I'd get us out of here. But... I'll give Gavin your necklace. I'll take Bella to observation. She'll know how brave her mama was."

He lifted Jan's canteen, still half-full, and drank a sip of it. The cool liquid coated his throat and took the edge off his thirst, filling him with relief. But all he felt was shame—shame that he could find relief while Jan sat next to him. Dead.

He tucked her oxygen pack in his work belt and forced himself to walk away—leaving her alone in the darkness. It wasn't her anymore. It was just a corpse. The Jan he'd known was gone.

Dritan squeezed into the crevice just as a tremor ripped through the cavern. Adrenaline surged through his veins. He braced himself against the rocks, pulse roaring in his ears as the cavern shook around him. Rocks hit the ground on either side of the crevice, rumbling their awful promise—that he'd be trapped here between the wall and rock—with no way out.

The quake ended, and Dritan called out in the direction of the main cavern. "McGill?"

No answer.

"McGill!"

Still no answer.

Dritan's muscles bunched up, and he breathed rapidly in the darkness, too terrified to push ahead, to find out if the rocks had trapped him here permanently.

None of us will make it out alive. Panic threatened to overtake him. Rescue hadn't come. Maybe Jan had been right. Maybe the president wanted them dead.

He'd failed Jan, and now he'd die just like she did, not able to keep any of his promises. And he'd failed Era, too.

Era had looked so devastated when he'd stepped onto the Soren transport. Her brown eyes had been tear-filled, despairing. He'd thought he could protect her from pain. But he was just a sub. How could he have been so stupid? His parents had died out in space, a hull breach repair gone wrong. No one could get to you fast enough out there. Now he'd suffocate, just as his parents had.

Dritan's eyes burned, and he rubbed at them. How would Era deal with his death? She'd been raised above the rest of them, protected. She didn't understand true deka society—the unspoken laws, the rules you had to follow. She hadn't grown up working the dangerous sublevels. She hadn't lost dozens of people the way he had.

Her father had been lead tech on the

London, and she'd fallen apart when he died. What would Dritan's death do to her? Who would take care of her this time? No one had ever needed him the way Era had.

Dritan closed his eyes and swallowed. He should just stay here in the crevice. Then, as his oxygen ran out, he could imagine the power core humming around him and pretend his death would be for the good of the fleet—that he'd been fixing something important in the sublevels.

But his death would mean nothing.

After you died in the fleet, you got to live on in the Infinitek way. The *Seattle* turned corpses into compost to make fertilizer for the *Meso*. But if he died down here, he'd just rot. And if they ever found his body, they'd incinerate it. That was the sick, disrespectful way they handled the dead on Soren.

A clear mind and determination keep men alive. His old crew leader's voice reverberated through his skull.

Clear mind. Determination. That's how subs survive.

How could he give up now, in the final hours? He couldn't quit. Not now. If death wanted him, he'd fight it every step of the way. He had to try to get out. To keep his promises.

Dritan took a deep, sputtering breath and pushed out toward the other side of the crevice. He barely breathed as he extended his arm to check and see if the way was still open. It was half-blocked.

He tightened his grip on the edge of the boulder and propelled himself forward, lurching out of the space, dragging his body against jagged edges.

When he broke through to the other side, he choked out a laugh, relief flooding him that he'd escaped the crevice. But he still had to dig his way to the exit.

When he threw his helio into the air to search for McGill, his momentary relief faded.

McGill was right where he'd left him, but he wasn't awake. Dritan rushed over to him and knelt. Dritan shook him, but he didn't move. His oxygen pack had red-lined. It was gone, or nearly gone. Dritan clumsily retrieved Jan's oxygen from his belt and replaced it. He looked closely and saw McGill's chest still rose and fell.

"Wake up." Dritan shook him, but he didn't respond.

PARAGON

The bandages on his leg were soaked through, and drops of blood leaked from them, pooling beneath his leg, reminding Dritan of his failure to save Jan.

He took another drink of water, and the hollow space in his gut filled up with something new, something more powerful than fear, more powerful than anger or grief. This new strength surged through him, and he got to his feet and headed for the rock pile blocking the exit—blocking the path to the recyc fan Jan had believed would be there.

He would work for as long as his oxygen lasted—with or without McGill. He lifted a stone and dropped it to the ground.

You're not taking me today, Soren.

CHAPTER SEVENTEEN

Tadeo stood in Central corridor beside Chief as the squads arrived, lining up along the wide corridor outside Central. The only sound in the silence was the squeaking of dozens of boots on smooth tile.

But his heart beat a staccato rhythm in his chest, so loud he was sure someone else must notice. He took a swig of his water to cool his dry throat. There was a bomb on the *Paragon*. There had to be. What sort of damage would five canisters of Artex and a canister of Zenith do?

Whatever thrill he'd experienced over his own subterfuge was long gone. This was serious now—and it was too late for him to waver from his chosen path to protect his mother.

Tatiana might be dead, but her actions could bring his whole family down with her. He had to find this bomb, and find a way to protect his family from the fallout, no matter what happened next.

Omar and Kiva stood in the squad at the front, their expressions stiff, unreadable. Sweat beaded on their foreheads, but if any of the guards were experiencing anxiety over what they'd heard or seen, none showed it.

When each of the ten squads—eighty men in all—had lined up in formation, Chief called them to attention.

Every guard stood taller, each pair of eyes trained on Chief and Tadeo.

"There may be a bomb on this ship," Chief said, "and if there is, we're going to find it."

Tadeo saw a flicker of fear pass over a few faces, but it was quickly squelched.

"The substance you are looking for may be mixed in a plasstex container, probably clear. It's the only grade that will melt under high heat and activate Zenith and Artex. The powder will look gray beneath the plasstex. Artex is black, and Zenith appears as larger white crystals mixed in."

"When heat is applied to Zenith and Artex, the bomb will explode. You will know the Zenith has been activated by heat if the white powder glows. And then you'll only have a few minutes before the explosion happens. It cannot be deactivated once activated. If that happens, we must get it off this ship as soon as possible."

Now a few murmurs rose up from the ranks, but a stern glare from Chief quieted them once more. "It won't get that far," he said. "We'll find these explosives and dispose of them. You are to tell no one what you know or what you are searching for. You will finish searching every job the terrorists did while aboard this ship, and we've chosen a handful of trusted maintenance workers to aid your search. You'll report to me or Lieutenant Raines if you find anything. Do not attempt to handle the explosives without us present. Do you understand?"

A chorus of 'Yes, sirs' filled the corridor.

Tadeo and Chief stepped out of the way as the squads began their march down the corridor—toward the sectors each had been assigned to search.

Kiva, Omar, and the rest of the president's personal squads stayed behind.

"You will go to command level and escort the board members to executive sector for a meeting," Chief said. "Protect them at all costs. I will meet you there to escort the president. Sergeant Omar, you lead. I need Lieutenant Raines with me."

Omar nodded and gestured, and all of them marched down the corridor after the others toward the stairwell.

Chief headed toward exec sector, and Tadeo walked fast to keep up, until they reached the double doors that separated the rest of guard level from executive sector.

Chief ran his shift card over the scanner, and the doors slid open, exposing the empty corridors beyond. "The executive sector is the only sector we know for sure is safe," Chief said. "We did a sweep after we airlocked the traitors. But I want you to do another sweep. Check behind every panel before the meeting starts. The president wants us both there, but I need to brief her first."

"Are we looking for a traitor from the *Perth*?"

"No. Zenith's made on the *Beijing*,

and Artex is made on the *Perth*. It's too dangerous to manufacture them together on the same deka. I think we're looking at a *Moscow* traitor. Someone from supply got a hold of this. Maybe traitors on the *Beijing*."

Tadeo swallowed back a bitter taste in his mouth. "Sir, you keep saying *Perth* colonists couldn't have done this, but... McGill was from the *Perth*. Maybe—"

Chief halted and pressed his index finger into Tadeo's chest, making his suit stick to him. "I told you never to speak of McGill."

"Yes, sir."

Chief searched Tadeo's face. Then, apparently satisfied, continued on to the conference cubic.

Lume bars glinted off shiny new panels at the end of the exec corridor. This was the spot where the hull breach had happened less than two weeks ago, after the terrorists had sabotaged the panels. The breach had taken on a new meaning now that he knew his mother's spy had sabotaged it.

Tadeo swallowed. "What kind of damage could this amount of Artex and Zenith do?"

The chief swiped his shift card before the executive conference cubic and looked at

Tadeo. His face had gone pale, and beads of sweat had collected on his forehead. "That much could take out more than a few levels. If you put it in the right place, it could cripple the ship beyond repair."

"Would you need special knowledge only a mining worker would have?"

"No," Chief said. "You just combine them together and apply high heat. That's it. If someone wanted to make a bomb and knew nothing, this would be the best way to do it. During the meeting, you stand—you don't sit. And you don't say one word unless the president directly asks you a question. And if the board asks about your mission, you leave Era out of it. Focus on the terrorists. That's an order. Now search this cubic."

The chief hurried out, and Tadeo took a deep breath, looking around the cubic. A wide table took up the center of the room, and a holo screen filled one wall. He needed to be looking for the explosives, not stuck in this room. Yet... yet he'd wanted to be invited into this room since the day he'd arrived.

The most important decisions in the fleet were made here. Right here at this table, they decided the fate of every colonist on every deka. The captains had their own laws, but they had to follow any laws made here or risk losing command.

Could his mother be right? Did everyone have spies on every ship? Was no one to be trusted?

Tadeo licked his lips and pulled off the first panel. He could never let anyone discover the link between Tatiana and his mother. It would mean forfeiting his mother's life. And if they learned he knew the truth...

It would mean forfeiting his own.

Tadeo finished checking the last wall panel before the first board member arrived. Then he stood in the corner of the room, back straight, and waited. Sweat soaked through the underarms of his suit, and his hair stuck to his forehead.

A faint beep sounded from the scanner outside the door, and it slid open. Tomas Nielsen, representative of the *Meso* and the *Oslo*, strode through the door. His broad shoulders took up the frame, and he peered at Tadeo from over a beaked nose, scowling as he took a seat.

"You going to tell me what's happening?" Tomas asked, folding his hands on the table.

"Sorry, sir. I'm not at liberty to say."

"I guess I should expect Nyssa to invite an inexperienced half to the meeting."

Tadeo fought to keep his expression blank. Tomas knew exactly who Tadeo was, yet he'd been rude to him each of the few times he'd ever addressed him.

The door slid open again, and Farida Mittal, representative for the *Perth* and *London*, and Jon Lau, representative for the *Kyoto* and *Beijing*, walked in.

Farida was shorter than Tadeo but several inches taller than Lau. Her youth and beauty were a stark contrast to his age and girth. Her long space-black hair was pulled away from her face, and she wore a strained expression. Did she know about the bomb? They all seemed to be uninformed. Otherwise, they'd be in a panic, no doubt.

Tomas grunted as the two took their seats. "About time you showed up."

"We're not late." Jon ran a hand over his ample stomach and gave Farida an annoyed look.

The door opened again, and Nyssa, Chief, and Nassef Yasin, representative of the *Dubai* and *Moscow*, strode in.

Nyssa took her seat at the head of the table, and Chief stood against the wall behind her. Nyssa's face was pale, and she looked exhausted, like she hadn't slept since Tadeo had last seen her.

Nassef sat beside Farida and tapped his long fingers against the tabletop. He was dark-featured and tall, taller even than Tadeo. He was an imposing man, whose face was impossible to read. If he already knew about the explosives, he wasn't showing it.

There were six chairs, and one was still empty.

Nyssa cleared her throat. "Where's Nicolas?"

Tomas snorted. "Probably passed out in his drink."

"We'll wait a few more minutes."

"Everyone who matters is here," Tomas said.

"It's important we're all together when I tell you why I've called this meeting," Nyssa said, folding her hands before her.

Tomas scowled again and folded his arms across his chest.

They waited a few more moments for the *Vancouver* and *Seattle* representative, and finally, the door slid open, and Nic Gonzalez stumbled through. His normally tan skin looked gray beneath the lume bars. As he took his seat near the corner where Tadeo stood, the scent of stale sweat and quin liquor wafted over.

Tomas pointed a finger at Nic. "This is the last time you come to a board meeting drunk."

"I'm not drunk."

"You—"

"Stop." Nyssa pounded a fist on the table and everyone looked to her. "This is not caretaker sector. And I won't put up with this."

Tomas grumbled but shut up. Nicolas screwed the cap back on his canteen.

"One hour ago," Nyssa said, her voice hard, "we found empty containers of explosives beneath the wall panels in paired sector. The terrorists we airlocked were planning something. We may have a bomb on this ship."

CHAPTER EIGHTEEN

Voices erupted around the table, everyone shouting at once. Only Nassef stayed silent, his face a blank mask. Tadeo took a deep breath and pressed his back into the corner.

Tomas grew red-faced and shouted above the rest. "How did this happen?"

Nicolas made to stand. "I'm getting my family off this ship. You knew about this yesterday—"

"I didn't."

"Then why did you halt the transports?"

Nyssa narrowed her eyes. "No one's going anywhere. Sit down, Nic, and listen to me."

Nicolas sank into his chair and pinched the skin between his brows. "You have five minutes."

"Why did it take so long to notify us of this?" Jon asked. "We should have known immediately."

"We just found the explosives," Nyssa said. "We know the terrorists who caused the hull breach were behind this. We found the empty canisters hidden in one of their bunks and behind the panels of one of the jobs their crew did in paired sector."

Tomas slammed a fat hand on the table. "How did this happen? What's the extent of the threat?"

"We don't know if there *is* a bomb," Nyssa said. "And we don't know where the explosives are located yet. But if there is a bomb, or more than one... it could do a lot of damage. It could cripple the ship. We found five empty Artex canisters, and one empty canister of," Nyssa took a deep breath, "Zenith."

The table erupted again. Farida and Jon exchanged tense glances, and all eyes went to them.

"You could take out most of a deka with that much," Farida said, her face pale.

PARAGON

"The *Beijing* does not treat the manufacture and handling of Zenith lightly," Jon said. "I swear to you all, the only ship that gets it is the *Perth*. And they're the ones responsible for sending it to Soren."

Nicolas leaned toward Farida. "The damn *Perth*. Can't you control your people? They're trying to blow us all down to that bloody red planet."

Chief looked at Nicolas like he'd like to send him and his accusations about the *Perth* down to the planet.

Farida gripped the edge of the table, her knuckles turning white. "And I can *assure* you, we don't have traitors on the *Perth*. The Artex and Zenith canisters are well-guarded and fully accounted for. If I knew anything about this," Farida said carefully, "Nyssa would have been the first person I told."

"Of course." Nicolas unscrewed his canteen for another swig. "And you two probably would have kept it from the rest of us."

"You're useless." Tomas reached out and tried to tear the canteen from Nic's grasp but failed. A splash of its contents landed on the table, and the sour scent of quin liquor filled the space. "Put that kak away."

"Have we questioned everyone on the crews the terrorists worked with?" Jon asked.

"There isn't anyone left to question." Nicolas spat, glaring at Tomas. "You all voted to send them to die on Soren."

"Yes," Nyssa said, her voice strong, cutting through room. "As we *agreed*, all the crews involved with the terrorists were sent to Soren. And everything's been taken care of. Just after our last meeting, I received word that all the crews we sent down on that transport were lost to a cave-in."

Everyone around the table exchanged glances, and Tomas drove a finger down at the table. "While we waste time up here, what's being done to find the explosives?"

Nyssa gestured toward the chief. "Chief Petroff, please brief us."

Chief stepped forward and kept his eyes straight ahead, not looking at any of them. "My recommendation is that the board and president evacuate until we track down the explosives. Right now, squads are searching every job the terrorists did. Then we'll search the rest of the ship. And we're investigating potential traitors in imports and exports. We've been bringing them up to Central for questioning, but with hundreds of workers on zero deck, this will take some time."

Jai Florian worked in imports. Tadeo had a name. He could speak up, tell them about what he'd found. But he wouldn't. They'd turn on him and his mother in an instant, the same way they turned on one another.

"We need an immediate lockdown of this ship. And if you're investigating imports," Tomas said, "what about the supply deka? The *Moscow* isn't trustworthy. We've caught them too many times feeding the black market."

Everyone turned to Nassef at the accusation against one of his ships. He crossed his hands before him, stoic despite the attention. "Tomas is wise to consider a lockdown," Nassef said, his deep voice low and even. "And if the *Moscow* had any hand in this, I can promise all of you, the perpetrators will face swift justice."

Nassef leaned back in his chair, looking unperturbed by the entire situation.

"That's it." Nicolas said. "I'm getting my son and wife and we're leaving on a transport. I'll be on the *Vancouver* waiting this out."

The president laid a hand on Nic's shoulder. "We don't even know—"

"You don't know much," Jon said. "I'm with Nicolas on this. I need to get my family to safety. There could be more terrorists aboard—they could set off a bomb at any moment."

"You're going to let terrorists scare us off our own damn ship?" Tomas asked. "We need to hunt them down—not flee."

"No transports have been given clearance to leave or board this ship," Nyssa said, her voice harsh. She still clutched Nic's shoulder tightly and pressed him back into his chair. "And this meeting is not over yet."

"We've been orbiting Soren for too long," Tomas said. "That's why we have this unrest. This is *your* doing, Nyssa."

"I did not give you leave to speak, Tomas," Nyssa said, challenging him with a direct gaze. Nyssa stepped away from Nic and wiped her hands together. "Lieutenant Raines, do you have any leads? Brief us on what you've discovered."

Tadeo stiffened as every pair of eyes settled on him. Only one thought raced through his mind. *My mother sent Tatiana to spy on you.* If he said it, they would turn on her. Convict her and airlock *her* for treason.

"Lieutenant Raines?" Nyssa snapped.

Tadeo stood tall. "President Sorenson, my squads found the canisters, and we're cross-referencing data to help Chief's search in imports and exports. If terrorists remain on this ship—we'll find them." Tadeo's voice came out deep, full of confidence he didn't feel. "I think the terrorists are or were targeting you, just like they were with the hull breach. I agree with Chief's recommendation for evacuation. You should all get off this ship until we've located the explosives and removed any and all threats to your persons."

Nyssa pressed her lips together in a thin, pale line, and Nassef leaned back in his chair, considering Tadeo. He stepped back into his corner and stared over the top of their heads, his chest tight. He was a liar, holding back information they needed. But they seemed to suspect nothing.

"I'm not running away," Tomas said. "Do you realize what that will look like? How the colonists will respond if we just abandon the ship and leave them all behind?"

"But, Tomas," Nassef said, his voice smooth, "the *Meso* and *Oslo* need your leadership. All of our dekas need us. And if we're the targets, perhaps removing ourselves will dissuade these terrorists from setting off their bomb."

Tomas nodded, but he looked uncertain now. "The *Meso* and *Oslo* do need my advocacy."

"They absolutely *rely* on your advocacy."

Tadeo's nostrils flared. Amazing how Nassef managed to calm Tomas... with transparent lies. Did either of them really believe that kak—that the *Meso* wanted his "advocacy"?

Nyssa stood, and the lume bar above brought out the deep hollows beneath her eyes. "We're the most likely targets of an attack. Command level will be cleared until the chief can locate the explosives. It's settled then. You will evacuate."

"And you? You can't stay here," Farida said. "You can come with me to the *London*. They'll take good care of us there, until we can come back."

"Oh, you want us to leave so you can gain full control over this ship? Over the guard?" Tomas said, his voice rising.

Nyssa leaned toward him, locking eyes with him. "I already *have* full control over this ship and the guard, Tomas. You'd be wise to remember that." She looked at the rest of them. "This meeting is adjourned. Get your families and belongings quickly and quietly, then get to the hangar bay. My guard will escort you. I'll ensure transports are ready within the half hour."

The board members got to their feet and filed out the door, but Tomas stuck around until the other four had gone through. When it was his turn to leave, he pointed at Nyssa.

"The Paragon hasn't faced this many problems in over a century," he said. "I'm leaving because the *Meso* and *Oslo* need me. But when we get back, there *will* be changes, and you *will* support them. We've replaced presidents before. Don't think we can't do it to you."

Nyssa took a few steps in his direction and stopped an inch from his face. "We've replaced board members before, too. Don't think I won't do it to you."

Tomas's face reddened, and they stared at each other for another moment. Finally, he broke eye contact and strode from the room.

The door slid shut, and Nyssa turned to the chief. Her shoulders caved a little as she went to him and rested her hand on his chest. The chief reached down and caressed her sleeve.

Tadeo's brows went up, and he stiffened. Had they forgotten he was still here?

"You have to take Tesmee and leave," the chief said, his voice rough. "Go with Farida."

"They can't use fear tactics on me. The colonists on this ship are *my* responsibility."

"You have to do it for Tesmee."

"I'm not putting Tesmee on a transport," she said.

"She's in more danger here than on the *London*." The chief cupped Nyssa's chin in one hand. "No one expects you to go there."

The chief and Nyssa? Tadeo wasn't sure whether to be shocked or repulsed. Chief was far below her station... but it wasn't like someone as old as Nyssa would pair again after losing a husband. At least this explained why she trusted Chief so much. As the two of them stared into each other's eyes, Tadeo shifted, uncomfortable. They definitely seemed to have forgotten his presence in the corner of the cubic. He cleared his throat, and the chief jerked his hand away from the president. She whirled to face Tadeo, her cheeks flushed.

"Chief is right," Tadeo said. "If there are still terrorists on this ship, you'd be their number one target. If you're not here—

maybe they won't set off the bomb. You might protect this ship best by leaving."

Nyssa stared at the tile floor for a long moment and then straightened her shoulders. "Then I'll do it. I'll take Tesmee and go."

"We'll keep everyone on their levels until you get out," Chief said, his face stern, fully himself again. "No one will be allowed in the stairwell. Raines, grab the files you've been cross-referencing. Then meet me on zero deck. Once the president and board are off the ship, we'll fast-track the questioning in imports and exports."

"You are both authorized to use *any* means necessary to locate these explosives," Nyssa said, her usual demeanor returning.

"Any means?" Chief asked.

"Yes. *Any* means necessary. Get the drugs. If you find anyone who may have been working with the terrorists, you do whatever you need to do to uncover the details of this plot and the location of the bomb. We'll clean up the mess when I get back."

∞

One name cycled through Tadeo's mind as he headed back to Central for his data. *Jai Florian.* He had to meet up with Chief on zero deck, so he had to move quickly and make sure there was no link between his mother, the terrorists, and the single *Meso* transfer who worked in imports.

Tadeo entered the cubic where he'd left Kiva working earlier and got his holo gear ready. He moved Kiva's handheld beside his own and manually connected the two so he could access her search results and cross-reference them with the archive data Mali had given him.

He twisted his wrist, and dual holo screens appeared before him.

"Jai Florian," he said.

Jai's records appeared. He opened Kiva's files to the list of the traitors' shift card access dates and dragged them into his handheld's holo screen.

"Cross-reference new shift card access dates and times with Jai Florian's shift card access dates and times."

If any of the traitors had ever been anywhere *near* Jai Florian, this should reveal that.

Both screens whited out, and a silver infinity symbol spun through the air. After a moment, Jai's schedule reappeared. At least a dozen of his shifts were highlighted.

Matches. Jai had been working in imports when one of the traitors had also been on zero deck. But it could just be a coincidence.

His heart pumped harder as he leaned forward and tapped each match, selecting them all. He splayed his hands wide and a third screen appeared, overlaying the original.

Match: Jai Florian; Tatiana Carizo

Tadeo's heart stopped. In the past ten months, Jai and Tatiana had both accessed the same sector of zero deck. They'd both gone to a spot near exports over a dozen times within an hour of one another.

Tadeo needed to find out if supplies from the *Meso* had come in on those days. He pinched his index finger and thumb together to extract the matches and placed them on his main holo screen. Then he went back to Kiva's files.

"Find date matches for *Meso* imports and exports."

Six matches in the past few months. Each time, a shipment had arrived from the *Meso*, via the

Moscow supply transport. On each of these days, Tatiana had entered the same sector as Jai, and later that day, a shipment had left the *Paragon* for the *Meso*.

A thrill shot through Tadeo, and he glanced toward the door. "Match dates with Jai Florian's imports sector access," he whispered.

The list populated, and Tadeo scanned down it, his heart thumping faster by the second.

Day 133 SHIFT LOG: Jai Florian - Imports Sector 1.4, First Shift, Second Shift. Hours 09:00-18:00

09:00 SHIFT CARD ACCESS: Jai Florian Imports Sector 1.4

10:45 SHIFT CARD ACCESS: Tatiana Carizo Zero Deck Sector 6

11:00 SHIFT CARD ACCESS: Jai Florian Zero Deck Sector 6

14:32 SHIFT CARD ACCESS: Jai Florian Exports Sector 5

16:30 EXPORT LOG: Exports Sector 5 - Meso shipment scanned out.

What stared back at him was damning. It was the same pattern four times. His mother's spy had been meet- ing up with Jai Florian. This was *proof.* Tadeo's mother had said Tatiana had a way to send her information. Jai had to have been helping her ship illegal comms.

Did that mean Jai still worked for his mother? Could he have helped smuggle the explosive powder aboard? This was bad. Everything kept leading back to his mother, but he couldn't believe she would ever put this ship in danger on purpose. Or put him in danger.

Tadeo shoved his handheld into his suit and jumped out of his chair.

The president could never find out about any of this, which meant he had to get to Jai before the chief did.

CHAPTER NINETEEN

Tadeo jogged down the stairwell to zero deck, running his hand along the smooth, worn banister. He was sweating freely now, but he didn't bother wiping it away.

The president had said they could use any means necessary to find the bomb. It was forbidden to even acknowledge the existence of the "encouragement" vials, but Tadeo had heard whispers about them from the veteran guards in the president's personal squads even before he'd seen Chief carry the case into Era's interrogation.

One dose caused the lungs to seize up for several seconds and made people feel like they'd been spaced. Every dose after that got stronger, the effects lasting longer. The strongest one was rumored to cause death.

What would Jai confess if the drugs were used on him? Tadeo couldn't let it come to that.

He walked through the double doors into the wide corridor of zero deck, straight past helio sector to the far side of the ship, and just as he reached imports and exports the buzzer called an end to second shift. *Kak.* He activated his eyepiece and found the image of Jai.

"Transparent mode," he said. "Activate facial recognition."

The main corridor split here, and tired colonists began to file out of doors on every side of him. His holo screen searched the passing colonists for matches as he looked at the sector numbers engraved in the metal panels, seeking Jai's sector.

Imports: Sector 1.4

He hurried down the corridor, pushing past the flood of colonists leaving cubics, trying to scan every face he passed. A few seemed frightened to see him there, but all of the colonists carefully avoided meeting his gaze and tried to keep their heads down. Would the software even find Jai in this crowd?

PARAGON

The double doors of Sector 1.4 slid open as he reached them, and workers began to file out. A mass of them crowded around the exit, waiting for their turn to scan their cards and check out for the day. He pushed past and stepped just inside, pressing his back to the wall.

Towering pallets of shipping containers lined the massive space in deep rows, and a few helios traveled down distant aisles with their owners. Each metal case contained goods imported from different dekas—the symbol of each ship stamped on the sides of the crates.

Tadeo kept his eyepiece trained on the colonists, his heart beating fast. Jai had to be somewhere in this crowd.

Tadeo's wristband crackled. Chief was comming him.

"Raines."

"We're clearing the stairwell now," Chief said, his voice coming through faint in Tadeo's earbud, "and we're going to come down stairwell C in five minutes so we can lead the president and board out safely. Where are you?"

"I'll be to zero deck soon," Tadeo lied.

"I'm about to head up to command to escort them down. Meet us in fifteen at C—we may need more help clearing the corridors."

Tadeo's holo screen blinked, and his eyes went to the dot overlaying the scene before him. Facial recognition had found a match. The dot blinked on the face of a short man with a dusky complexion and black hair. He stood at the edge of the crowd, on the opposite side from Tadeo.

Jai Florian. Match: 100%

"Raines?" Chief said.

One chance. He had this one chance to find out what Jai knew about his mother before the chief talked to him. Jai scanned his shift card and headed into the corridor.

"Yes, sir."

Tadeo switched off his comm and pushed through the crowd, in search of Jai. *There.*

He walked up beside the short man who glanced up at Tadeo and stumbled right into the wall panel. Tadeo grabbed him by the arm and led him a little further down the corridor, to the first cubic he saw.

"What... what's this about? I'm scheduled for questioning tomorrow."

"Not anymore."

Colonists openly stared at them as Tadeo pulled his shift card from his pocket and scanned it across the cubic's scanner.

"This is a storage cubic—"

"Good," Tadeo said.

The door opened, and Tadeo pushed Jai inside and stepped in after him. Lume bars lit up the cramped space as the door shut behind them. Narrow shelves lined the cubic, filled with bins of bolts and tools.

"What's going on?" Jai gripped the shelf beside him, his hand shaking. "What do you want?"

Tadeo carefully removed his eyepiece and placed it and his handheld on the shelf beside him. His heart rate sped up as he approached Jai.

The man's eyes widened, and he swallowed. "I—"

Tadeo slammed Jai to the ground and pressed his back into the chipped tiles. "Are you a terrorist?"

"What?"

"Answer me!"

The man shook, and Tadeo pressed him harder into the floor.

"No... I—"

"Did you work with Tatiana Carizo?"

The man went paler than hulled quin.

"Chief Petroff is on his way right now," Tadeo said. "What they're about to do to you is far worse than what I'm doing."

"I didn't know."

"You didn't know what?" Spittle flew from Tadeo's mouth and landed on Jai's cheek. "Did you aid the terrorists? Did you smuggle goods on and off this ship? Did you send comms illegally to the *Meso*?"

"No, I would never—"

"Who do you work for?"

Jai blinked rapidly and pressed his shoulders into the tile as if trying to escape through the floor. Then his expression brightened. "Wait. You're—you're Tadeo Raines."

Tadeo's breath caught, and he lifted him by the collar, then slammed him into the floor again. Jai groaned in pain.

"I know you worked with Tatiana," Tadeo said, his voice a low growl. "They'll airlock you for this. But if you confess before I turn you over to them... you might have a chance to survive all this."

Jai stared up at him, his face a twisted mask of fear.

Tadeo let go of the man in disgust and stood up. "Tell me what you know."

The man stumbled to his feet and took a few steps back, crashing into the shelf. "Trading's never been punishable by death. It's not treason."

Tadeo took a threatening step toward him. "Trading? Or aiding the black market?"

Jai licked his lips. "Tatiana came to me when she got here, asking for my help. But I swear I had nothing to do with what she—"

"I have evidence right now that links you with *all* the terrorists we airlocked."

"I didn't do nothin'!"

"I don't care about your little black market operation. You aided the terrorists."

He stepped toward Tadeo and grabbed his sleeve, his eyes pleading. "No. Please believe me, I had nothing to do with that hull breach. I'm just a go-between. I'm no traitor. I get things from imports, and I move them. Tatiana came to pick them up. Half the time, I don't even look at what I pass on."

Tadeo shrugged off the man's grasp. "And exports?"

Florian wiped at his mouth and shook his head. "Tatiana had me send cubes. Messages.

You gotta believe me. If I'd thought she was a traitor—"

"Listen to me carefully," Tadeo said, his voice low but harsh. "Other guards will be coming soon. You're going to tell me who you work for. Then you're going to tell me everything you ever gave Tatiana or sent her. Right now. Or the guards will torture it out of you. And then you'll be airlocked."

"I..."

"Who do you work for?" Tadeo slammed his hand into the man's chest, knocking him into the metal shelf again."

The man held up his hands, palms out. "Please—I'll tell you."

"Now."

Jai bit his lip and tried to move away from Tadeo, but there was nowhere to go. "I work for your mother, sir. Captain Raines of the *Meso*."

Tadeo's pulse quickened, and he took a step away from Jai, his stomach twisting. "If you're lying—"

"I'm not. I'm loyal to her—I'm loyal to *you*, sir. You have to believe me."

Bile rose in Tadeo's throat, because he *knew* in that moment that he'd kill this man himself if he had to—to protect his mother and her secrets.

"Tell me what you gave Tatiana," Tadeo said, his voice hard.

"I just hand over cases," Jai said. "I don't ask questions."

"From where?"

"From every deka... through the *Moscow*. I pull marked cases off the pallets and hand them to whoever asked for them. Tatiana... I think most of her cases came from the *Meso*. It's easy to hide things in the quin grain. No one checks."

Tadeo's throat tightened. "So... do people in supply on the *Moscow* put these illegal items in the cases? Or... or did Tatiana's shipments all come from the *Meso*? What did you give her?"

"I don't know who packages it. I always assumed it got packed on the *Meso*. And I don't look in every case. It was always just things like... like exec standard lavender soap or some soyad meant for command level."

"Is there anyone else here working for my mother?"

The man paused, then shook his head. "If there is, I don't know about 'em. Everything was for Tatiana. The other stuff I get, it's... it's just black market trading. Not like the arrangement I have with Captain Raines."

Arrangement. If the Artex and Zenith canisters had come in a quin crate, they might have come from the *Meso*. But how had explosive powder gotten on the *Meso* in the first place? And why would his mother send it here? Heat flooded Tadeo, and he got in Jai's face again.

"There might be a bomb on this ship right now. You'll be blamed—for giving Tatiana explosives."

Jai's mouth dropped, and his eyes went wild. "What? No!" His voice cracked. "I'd never give anyone that if I knew."

"Think carefully now—was there ever a time she got anything from a different ship?"

Jai squinted down at the tiles and rubbed his eyes. He wrapped his hands around his temples as if he were trying to extract his memories by force. Then his face jerked up. "A few days before... before the hull breach and her sentencing. The *Beijing*. She asked for something from there that wasn't on my list."

The *Beijing*. Where they manufactured Zenith. Tadeo grabbed the man by his suit again, and Jai blanched. "Another case?"

"Yes."

"I remember, because it was hard for me to get to. It was a tough job, but Tatiana worked for Captain Raines, and I was supposed to get her anything she asked me for."

"Why was it a tough job?"

"Because... the case she wanted was hidden in a shipment of power cell inserts."

Power cell inserts. Like the insert in Dritan's cubic.

"Why would inserts be hard to access?"

"Because they were meant for the power core. Hardly anyone could get near them."

The power core.

What had his mother said? Tatiana had done maintenance work in sensitive areas on the *Meso.* Silo sector, transports, command level, *power core.*

Tadeo released his hold on Jai's suit. "Turn around."

The man hesitantly turned, and Tadeo grabbed his wrists and cuffed both to the shelf.

"I thought you said if I—"

"Shut up. Don't talk. Don't move." Tadeo pushed his hair out of his eyes and grabbed his eyepiece and handheld from the shelf.

The power core on every ship was closely guarded and well-protected. Only a few maintenance crews had access, and all were carefully vetted. There was *no* way Tatiana could have gained illegal access. But... she knew her way around a core. She knew the safeguards. And if you wanted to plant a bomb somewhere where it could do the most damage... Exploding a bomb in the power core could blow up the entire ship.

Tadeo gestured with damp palms, bringing up the files he'd saved in his handheld.

He pulled up the shift card access for every one of the terrorists, Dritan, and Era. "Search shift card access to power core or any access on level P2."

A list of results popped up. The sublevel workers had accessed level P2 hundreds of times as part of their normal duties.

"Sort by proximity to power core entrance."

The list sorted, bringing up the cubics they'd entered near the entrance. Several identical entries appeared at the top. All Tatiana. She'd visited the same spot next to the corridor on dozens of occasions. In the final entry, she'd stayed there for over two hours, in the middle of a work shift, before she'd entered another corridor in P2.

Tadeo tapped the last entry, and the date appeared.

The morning after the hull breach—only days after the *Beijing* shipment would have arrived, Tatiana had spent two hours right next to the power core. If someone had met her there, their card wasn't showing up in his data.

Tatiana had been scheduled to fix an air recyc fan in caretaker sector with Samuel Smith, Jonas Keen, and Dritan Corinth that day. The work schedule claimed they'd all been there, that they'd all checked in with their shift cards. But Tatiana had left and gone to the power core. The traitors had covered for her.

Tadeo rested a hand on his pulsegun and whirled back to Jai. "You'll be the one to die for this, and I'm not letting you take my family down with you."

"But—but I'm loyal! What are you going to do?" Jai's eyes shone, and he darted a glance at Tadeo's gun. He tried to back further away, but the cuffs stopped him.

Tadeo's mind raced through the scenarios. Sending Jai out the nearest airlock. Pulsing him right here and dragging his body to the airlock to get rid of the evidence. But the corridor outside was teeming with people, so neither of those alternatives worked.

Plus, his mind was a mess—he wasn't thinking straight—and Chief wanted him at stairwell C.

Tadeo swallowed. "I should kill you. You know too much. But you're staying here for now. I'll come back when I decide what to do with you. You don't make a sound, you don't try to escape, and maybe I'll find a way to let you live..."

Dread filled Tadeo as he turned and left Jai cuffed in the room. This situation had suddenly spun far, far out of his control.

But none of it would matter if there *was* a bomb in the core, and he didn't get to it in time.

CHAPTER TWENTY

A deep voice woke Zephyr, and she knew *he* was in a rage, coming for her. She'd screwed up again, gotten in trouble. He would beat her, leave her bruised and broken, and her mother would look away—doing nothing—like always. Whatever Zephyr had done wrong, it wouldn't be worth the pain he'd inflict.

"Tell me again," the man demanded. "Why is this medic in here?"

Zephyr's eyes fluttered open, and she rolled off the metal bunk onto unforgiving tile.

"I don't know, sir. Lieutenant Raines brought her in here. For questioning, sir. I'm supposed to call him as soon as she wakes from sedation... which should be soon."

"You'll do no such thing," the deep voice said. "I'm comming medlevel. You're to release her back to their care immediately."

"Yes, sir."

Zephyr blinked against the bright lights and groaned at the pain shooting through her back. This wasn't her bunk, and she wasn't on the *London* anymore. Her father wasn't coming for her, but that realization didn't bring relief. She was still trapped.

She looked through the bars and saw Chief Petroff exiting the brig. "You get that medic out of here, Holt."

"Yes, sir. I will."

Zephyr peeled her palms from the tile. Her hands were covered in dried blood and small cuts. Even her forearms were spattered with sticky red-brown. Zephyr's chest lightened. Most of it was Paige's blood. *This* punishment was well-worth the crime. But she was done with Tadeo. *Kakface.* She was done with this ship and these people. As soon as she got out of there, she'd demand the president release her back to the *London*.

She flexed one hand, and bits of blood flaked off and drifted lazily to the floor.

Holt, the guard, approached the cell

beside hers. The old woman lying in it had been sleeping since Zephyr arrived. She was one of Tadeo's other prisoners. What could this ancient woman possibly have done wrong?

"Medic Faust," Holt said.

Medic Faust. That name sounded familiar. Why?

"Are you awake?"

"Yes," came the creaking reply. The woman was wearing the white, loose suit of a medlevel patient, not the light blue suit a medic ought to be wearing. Maybe she was sick.

"You should get up now. You're going back to hospice."

Not just sick, then. Dying. Wow, Tadeo really was screwed up. Why had he imprisoned an old, dying woman?

The gray-haired medic struggled to sit up on her bunk. "I'm aware. I do have ears, you know. Shall I collect my things?" She gestured around her cell, eyes wide, as if to point out just how empty it was.

Holt gave her an awkward nod before shuffling back to his place behind the counter.

Idiot. So many people on this ship were idiots. Medic Faust threw Zephyr an annoyed look, like she'd heard Zephyr's unspoken thought and agreed. Then she lay back down.

Medic Faust.

Era had said that name. After Dritan had left for Soren, Era had told her she needed to schedule her follow-up appointment with a Medic Faust.

The woman was from population management. This medic was the *reason* Era killed herself.

Zephyr jumped up from the floor and went to the bars separating the medic's cell from her own. The medic's bunk was within arm's reach, and Zephyr pulled on her suit through the bars.

"Medic Faust." Zephyr's voice came out rough. "Did you have a patient named Era Corinth?"

The medic's eyes opened. They were gray, the color of newly forged panels. She sat up and inched away from Zephyr. "I'm Nora. I'm no longer a medic."

"Were you Era's medic?" Zephyr repeated, her pulse buzzing in her ears.

Nora licked her lips and looked down at her hands. Her old skin was thin, and her veins protruded through. "I did provide care for that girl," she said quietly. Then she waved a hand, as if dismissing the thought of Era. "Just not well enough."

Zephyr's heart beat faster, and hate for the woman flooded her. "You know, she died because of you. She killed herself."

Nora met her gaze. "I know. But *I* didn't kill her."

"But it was *your* fault."

"I don't make the rules."

Zephyr fought to keep her breathing even and darted a glance at Holt. He was staring at them.

"You, two," Holt said. "You can't be talking in there."

Zephyr crouched down so her face was even with the medic's. "Did she ever say anything to you? Did she give you even the slightest hint she might want to kill herself because *you* were going to terminate her pregnancy?"

The medic's expression didn't change, and that made Zephyr want to throw the medic's failure in her face, make her ears ring with it until she died. "It's your job as a medic to prevent suicides—you should have kept her on medlevel—made sure she started the grimp."

Nora blinked slowly and nodded. She scooted an inch further away. After a long pause, she responded, her steely gaze meeting Zephyr's square on. "There are things in this fleet people would kill for. And things that people would die for."

"What? What do you mean?"

Nora laughed, and Zephyr's rage flared. She pushed her hand through the bars, trying to snatch at the medic's short gray hair, to rip it out until she felt the pain Zephyr felt.

The medic moved further away, avoiding Zephyr's grasp.

"Did Era say something to you?"

The medic gave a stiff nod but didn't respond.

"Tell me what she said."

"Does it matter?" Nora asked. "Your friend is gone."

"Did she—did you know she'd try to kill herself?"

The old woman stared out across the small cell, then swung her legs to the floor, wincing against the apparent pain the movement caused. "My biggest mistake has been knowing too much and doing too little. But here I am, still alive after all these years. And your friend... she's dead. Let that be a lesson to you."

"What..." Zephyr said, her voice rising, "did she *say* to you?" All of Zephyr's senses were on fire, and her skin felt as if a thousand-volt charge ran through it. She got to her feet and pressed herself closer to the bars.

There are things in this fleet people would kill for. And things that people would die for. What the medic was saying was important. Zephyr didn't know how she knew it—but she knew. And she desperately wanted to know what Era had said. Had she hinted to the medic that she'd planned to take her own life, even before they'd gotten news of Dritan's death?

"Tell me what you're talking about!"

The medic blinked like she'd forgotten Zephyr was there. "I won't."

"Kerrigan. Uh-Exec Kerrigan," Holt said, standing up. "Get back to your bunk."

Zephyr stared him down, and his pale, freckled skin reddened.

The door to the brig slid open, and two blue-suited medics carrying a stretcher entered.

Panic surged through Zephyr, making her sick, and she banged on the bars. This woman knew something about Era's last days. Something Zephyr didn't. Tears pricked her eyes. "Please. Just tell me what Era said. I need to know."

Nora pursed her lips. "She said nothing to me. Nothing at all."

The medics spoke with Holt, and he came over to Nora's cell, keys jangling.

"What is *wrong* with you?" Zephyr asked, yelling again.

"You're right." Nora said, just as loudly. She nodded and stared at Holt as he unlocked her cell. "This does need to end. But I'll be dead in a few weeks or months. And it will all end with me."

Zephyr stepped away from the bars as the medics entered the cell and began to help Nora onto the stretcher. Era probably hadn't said anything. The old woman sounded crazy—out of it from power core sickness or her meds.

The medics carried her off in a stretcher, and when they were gone, Zephyr dragged herself back to her bunk. She slid to the floor in front of it and rubbed her hands together to get the dried blood off.

Nothing made sense. She tried to

stay calm and focused on taking even breaths, but something tugged at her, preventing her from numbing her chaotic emotions again.

Her father always said that if you let your emotions get in the way, you'd never survive life in the fleet. He said feelings were the reason accidents happened, the reason the deka riots and shortages happened. That when people felt too freely, they became a burden to the fleet.

But he was *wrong*. Sometimes emotions told you things your mind couldn't. And her mind was telling her *not* to numb herself, that her emotions had something important to say. So she let them wash over her, and she sat with the burning pain and let it take her.

And for the first time since yesterday, since the awful moment Tadeo said Era killed herself, Zephyr's mind cleared, even while her heart ached. Each moment in the past three days crystallized in her mind—sharply outlining the shape of all that had come before.

Everyone was wrong about Era's death. It made perfect sense for her to kill herself, but Zephyr knew Era, and she *wouldn't* just do that.

Had Medic Faust been delirious from the meds?

There are things in this fleet people would kill for... and die for.

Zephyr remembered the night Era died—each moment as it had played out, despite how fresh the pain was.

After they got the news that Dritan had died in the cave-in, Era had been hysterical. But she'd been trying to speak through her sobs. Her pain had broken Zephyr—she'd wanted to make it go away—so she'd forced Era to swallow the grimp.

What had Era been trying so hard to tell her?

Zephyr closed her eyes. Era had said something about the defect... that it was a *lie*. She'd said something about treason, too. Maybe she'd been talking about the hull breach, about the traitor who'd tried to kill Tesmee. Zephyr had assumed Era was losing it, saying nonsensical things.

Then the grimp took hold, and Era had fallen asleep before explaining what she meant.

Something wasn't right about any of this. But what? What had really happened that night? When had Era awoken and decided to take her own life?

Zephyr gasped and sat up straight,

clenching her sticky hands into tight fists.

Era had said something *else* between her sobs. *"I recorded the truth. Hid it."*

"She tried to tell me," Zephyr whispered. "But I wouldn't listen."

Zephyr covered her mouth, inhaling the coppery-salt-scent of dried blood, and leaned back against the bench. The hard edge of it cut into her scalp, and her eyes watered. What truth had Era hidden? It seemed absurd—Era had shared everything with Zephyr, hadn't she?

She said she'd recorded something and hidden it. Was she hysterical, or did a recording really exist somewhere? And could it hold the answer to why she'd committed suicide?

Zephyr wiped the tears from her eyes and leaned forward, staring through the bars of her prison.

If Era had hidden a last message somewhere, Zephyr was going to find it.

CHAPTER TWENTY-ONE

By the time Tadeo reached stairwell C, guards were already pouring out, filling up the corridor. He caught sight of Omar and Kiva in the press, as the squads lined up on both sides of the corridor, hands on their weapons.

Nicolas Gonzalez, Jonathan Lau, Farida Mittal, and the families came out next. They had metal cases with them, and their faces were drawn with fear. Tomas came with his wife and daughter next, a scowl on his face, and Nassef and his family followed.

The president was the last to exit, flanking Tesmee on one side with the chief on the other.

Tadeo edged around the board to get to the chief and president.

"Chief!"

Chief's brow furrowed, and he paused in the orders he was giving to the squad.

"Say it quick. What is it?"

"I found something in the data," Tadeo said, keeping his voice low.

"What did you find?"

"I think the bomb might be in the power core."

Nyssa gasped and pulled Tesmee closer.

Chief's nostrils flared. "Why do you think that?"

"Tatiana Carizo spent a lot of time in a cubic close to the power core. And the morning after the hull breach—she left work to go there. I don't know if she met someone, but—"

"That doesn't mean the bomb's in the power core," Chief said, irritated. "It's impossible to get anywhere near it without access. The terrorists had none."

"But what if they did? What if they have someone working with them—on the inside?"

Nyssa stepped closer. "No, everyone's clean. There are strict regulations about who works down there."

"I need to look into it," Tadeo said. "Tatiana worked the power core on the *Meso* before she transferred here. She knew all the safeguards, all the protocols, all about the regulations. Maybe someone in the power core helped the terrorists. I don't know, but if you wanted to take out a ship, wouldn't that be the best place to put a bomb?"

Nyssa shook her head and squeezed Tesmee's arm. "The terrorists would have died with us."

"What if this was their plan if the hull breach failed?"

The chief shook his head and cast a glance at the board members, who were trying to listen in. "We need to get them out of here."

Blood rushed in Tadeo's head. "Just let me take a few men down there to question the power core workers."

Chief nodded and glanced down the corridor, clearly eager to move. "Take them. I need to get these people to safety. If you find anything, comm me."

Tadeo grabbed Kiva, Omar, and two others and led them back into the stairwell.

"What's going on, sir?" Kiva asked.

"We think the bomb might be in the power core."

Kiva gasped and went pale. The others, including Omar, looked stricken, sick.

"I think someone in the power core could've been working with one of the terrorists," Tadeo said, rushing to get the words out. "Be on the lookout for suspicious behavior while we're questioning the workers."

"Yes, sir," they said in unison. All of them wiped the fear from their faces and stood taller.

"Let's go."

∞

Tadeo raced through the corridors of P2, his veins pulsing with fresh adrenaline, his guards at his back.

The hum of the power core grew as they neared it, and Tadeo fought back memories of Era—and the airlock. They were heading toward it, but when they reached the final corridor, they turned left, away from it, and Tadeo felt the pressure in his chest ease up. All that mattered right now was finding the explosives. He hoped he was wrong about all of this—that Tatiana'd had some other reason for coming down here.

Another few minutes brought them to the main power core entrance. Tadeo didn't have access here. The chief did. So did the board members and a few trusted sublevel workers. Could one of them be a terrorist?

Tadeo scanned his shift card at the cubic adjacent to the massive doors. The cubic door opened, revealing two men and a woman sitting at a table. The woman jumped up, holding a tray, and tried to conceal it behind her back. It was food brought down illegally from the galley.

"Who's in charge here?" Tadeo shouted to compete with the hum of the power core.

The oldest man stood up and came to the door. Light scars crisscrossed his face, and his shaved head made him look older than he probably was. "I am," he said.

"And you are?"

"Sorry, sir. I'm Gavin Lanar."

"Lanar, I have some questions for you. Clear the room."

Lanar gestured to the other two, and the woman sheepishly dropped the tray back onto the table and exited the cubic with the man.

Tadeo pulled Omar and Kiva aside. "Watch them. See how those two act. Don't let them go anywhere."

Then he went into the cubic and shut the door behind him. "Sit down, Lanar."

"What is this about, sir? I already reported in and said there won't be another power outage—I got more guys coming down to help fix the generator tonight. We finally got the parts..." He trailed off at whatever look was on Tadeo's face.

"Terrorists may have planted explosives somewhere in or around the power core," Tadeo said.

Lanar's jaw dropped, and Tadeo studied him. He seemed to be genuinely shocked. "That's impossible. We're the only ones with access. But even if there were explosives, it would take a lot to blow through that hull. A lot."

"A lot like a combination of Artex and Zenith?"

Lanar's face went ashen. "Yes."

Tadeo leaned over the table, getting

close to Lanar's face. "One of the terrorists smuggled Artex and Zenith onto this ship. If someone wanted to blow up the power core, where would they place the explosives?"

Lanar swallowed and shook his head. "The plasma field is encapsulated. You can't just blow it up, or even get near it. You'd have to place a charge right up against it, and the only things touching that hull are..."

"Are what?"

"The power cell inserts."

A thrill ran through Tadeo, and he began to pace the small cubic. The inserts again. It meant something.

"What are they used for?"

Lanar blinked and rubbed a hand over his shaved head. "They cover the outside hull. Our generators use them to draw power from the core."

"How many inserts are there?"

"Over eight thousand. One hundred cells per generator."

Eight thousand. It'd take days or weeks to check them all. "Could someone place explosives inside the insert?"

"Maybe, but... It gets nearly hot enough in there to melt the insert itself."

Heat activated Zenith. Tadeo grunted, frustrated. If the power cell inserts got that hot, there *couldn't* be explosives hidden there. The Zenith would have activated shortly after it was put in place, and it would have exploded already.

The power outages. Tadeo sucked in a breath and pounded his fist against the table, rattling the half-empty tray. "What's been causing the outages?"

Lanar's brow creased. "One of our generators is down. Every time the ship hits a certain power threshold, it causes a black-out, and we have to reboot everything."

"You said the generators draw power from the core through the inserts."

"Right."

"So the section with the bad generator is dead then?"

"Yes."

"If it's dead... how hot do the inserts get?"

Lanar's mouth dropped, and his eyes widened. "It's *cold*. The inserts in that section aren't functioning. They won't conduct power till that generator gets fixed."

"So if they *were* hidden there..." Tadeo's chest expanded, and a high sensation, *excitement*, ran through him. "They wouldn't have been triggered yet. We need to remove every one of those inserts."

Lanar stood up. "We can, but one problem. We have to use welding gear to get them out."

"Was welding gear used to install each one?"

"Yes."

Tadeo paused, thinking. It had to be done. If they'd used welding gear to install it, and the Zenith hadn't activated, they had to be able to get them out again. But if the explosives were in the core, who had put them there?

Tadeo narrowed his eyes at Lanar and studied him for a moment. "We're coming in with you."

Lanar led them a few doors down, into a large changing area lined with three radiation protection suits.

Lanar pointed along the far wall to another door. "We have extras in storage. Wes and Cind, show them how to gear up."

Tadeo looked at the other two power core workers as they led his guards to storage. One man, one woman. The woman, Cind, was even older than Lanar, with a serious expression and wary eyes. And Wes, slightly younger than Lanar with the same scars crisscrossing his face and arms, looked even more nervous than Cind and Lanar.

These were the kind of subs who worked years to prove their worth and loyalty before gaining access to an area as sensitive as the power core. If he'd met them under any other circumstance, he'd have taken them for the most loyal of colonists. If they were terrorists, they'd done a good job hiding it from everyone. But so had Tatiana.

Unless his mother *knew* what Tatiana was. Unless his mother had sent explosives to her for this very purpose.

Tadeo clenched his jaw tight. His mother had nothing to do with this plot. She wouldn't put an entire ship in danger. She wouldn't put *him* in danger like this.

"Lanar—how many power core workers are there?"

"Sixteen. Normally just three at night."

Tadeo nodded. So these three could be loyal. They'd have to question the rest.

Lanar began to pull one of the bulky suits over his maintenance suit.

"That one should fit you," Lanar said, gesturing to the suit on the hook beside it.

"Belonged to one of ours who just came down with the sickness."

Tadeo stepped into the bulky suit. "Space gear," he said, half to himself. He'd never worn space gear, never had to. The suit weighed at least thirty pounds. A few plump liquid oxygen packs lined the collar.

"Modified space gear for the radiation in there. Those packs will feed oxygen continually into your helmet for up to twelve hours in the core sector." Lanar pointed. "Helmet's shatterproof. Impermeable. The air gets toxic. And you don't want to leave your work belt or the comcuff on. The suit won't go on right. You can attach the helio and your shift card to the loops here," he said, pointing to the waist.

"How do you communicate in the power core? Isn't it too loud?"

"There are local comms in the helmets. They activate when you speak," he said. "Everyone with a suit will hear you."

Tadeo reluctantly pulled off his work belt, comcuff, and pulse gun and placed them on the metal bench. He'd have to leave one of the guards to watch the guns.

He finished zipping up his suit as his guard and the other workers came out of storage, fully geared up in the thick padded anti-radiation suits. They hadn't yet put on the helmets.

Kiva held everyone's work belt and holsters in her arms, and she and Omar came over to Tadeo.

"Lieutenant, can we have a word?" Kiva asked.

Tadeo stepped off to the side, and everyone pretended not to be watching or listening.

"The man," Omar said, his voice a rough whisper. "He's nervous—sweating. We gotta keep an eye on him."

"Alright," Tadeo said, forcing himself not to look in Wes's direction. "I'll watch him. Kiva, stay behind and guard the guns."

"But—"

"I trust you to do it. And comm Chief. Tell him we're searching the power cell inserts. And then I want you to comm me through the helmet comm the second Chief says the president and board are away."

Tadeo pulled his helmet over his head and secured it to his suit. Everyone else did the same, and Tadeo led his squad, only three strong now, including Omar, into the corridor. The subs followed.

"Can you all hear me?" Tadeo asked.

A chorus of "Yes, sirs" came back at him.

"There may be a bomb in the power core." Tadeo looked directly at Wes, then Cind to see how they reacted to his words. They both looked very afraid. Tadeo cleared his throat. "Specifically, there may be explosives hidden within the power core inserts on the outer layer of the hull. We have one hundred power core inserts to search. We're looking for a clear plasstex container filled with a black powder mixed with white crystals. Each of my guards will work with one worker as we search. A welding tool must be used to remove the inserts, but we have to be extremely cautious. Heating the explosives could cause them to detonate. I'm hoping we find nothing... but if we do find something, leave it right where it is. We have to call Chief Petroff. This entire ship could blow if we fuck this up."

Another chorus of "Yes, sirs" rang through his helmet, weaker this time. Faces filled with fear stared back at him from behind glasstex headgear. His guards fought to contain it, but this time, hiding it was impossible. Wes looked gray beneath his helmet, sweat beading on his brow.

Adrenaline coursed through Tadeo, making his pulse speed up. He gestured to Lanar. "We're ready to go in."

CHAPTER TWENTY-TWO

Lanar scanned his card, and the thick metal doors creaked open, slow and heavy. Heat rushed out at them as they stepped onto the core platform, and the doors closed behind them. The hum was deafening in this massive space.

Tadeo had never been allowed in here. Not with the threat of accelerating power core sickness.

Lume bars ran the length of the walls and ceiling, illuminating the space. He had to strain his neck to look up to the top of the power core. The metal curved away from them, the only hint that if he could see the entire thing at once he'd be seeing a giant metal globe. Like a helio whose glow no one would ever see. The plasma inside must look like a sun. It contained enough energy to last for hundreds of years—until the fleet reached New Earth. Unless someone blew a hole through the metal. If a bomb was here, it would definitely blow apart this entire ship.

Huge, dented machines ran along the wall closest to the platform they stood on, creating the hum heard throughout the sublevels. Tadeo could feel the blistering heat emanating off them even through his suit. Why had he always thought the heat came from the core itself? Thick wires the width of both Tadeo's legs ran from the generators up to sections of the power core.

Lanar and his team went to the side of the space and came back with handheld lasers.

The comm crackled in Tadeo's helmet.

"The cold sector is midway up," Lanar said. "We have to climb ladders and work from the scaffolding. Are you sure you want your guards up there, Lieutenant Raines? The core cycles every few minutes. It can get rough up on the corewalks. Everything vibrates, things slip. We'll be high up, and if you fall, you won't survive it. We've lost people, and they were experienced."

Tadeo walked closer to the power core. Scaffolding ran along the entire globe and disappeared over the ledge to the levels below this one, so workers could tend to the entire core.

"We're coming up," Tadeo said. "I'll follow Wes. Omar, you go with Lanar. Finnegan," he gestured to one of his last two guards. "Stay down here by the doors. The other follows Cind. And everyone, be careful."

Lanar led them to the ledge and fired off a list of numbers to his crew. They replied in the affirmative.

Lanar pointed upward. "The cold section is twenty feet up and spans one hundred inserts. Each of us will take a third." Lanar began to climb a ladder, and Omar followed. Cind led the other guard down the line.

Wes averted his eyes, not meeting Tadeo's gaze as he led him down the line to a ladder in the opposite direction.

He hooked his welding tool to a loop on his belt and started up the ladder. Tadeo waited a moment, then followed after him, his heart pounding. He'd climbed several rungs when he felt a rumble beneath his gloves.

The comm crackled. "Hang on," came Lanar's voice. "Cycle coming."

Wes halted above him, and Tadeo clutched the rungs more tightly. The rumble became a strong vibration as the magnetic field cycled within the core. He hung on for a moment more, not moving, and his body shook with the ladder. Tadeo looked down the curving body of the core, illuminated by lume bars the whole way. The view of the drop snatched his breath away. They were near the bottom portion of the globe, but it still went down at least a hundred feet. Lanar hadn't been kidding. A drop like that would kill a man.

A thrill raced through him as the vibration ceased. He took a deep breath, tasting the odd metallic bite of the packaged oxygen.

"It's over," Lanar said. "A few more minutes before it comes around again. Get in place. Deactivate your laser in between cycles. We don't want to risk setting an explosion off if there really is a bomb in here."

They continued their climb and reached the corewalk Wes had been heading for. Tadeo stepped onto the thin metal platform. Railings lined either side of it, and there was only room for Wes and him to stand side by side. He glanced around and saw Omar with Lanar on a corewalk to his right and Cind and Finnegan to his left.

This close to the core, Tadeo could see the power cell inserts. The long rectangles ran in even rows beside the corewalk. Rings of metal protruded from each rectangle, clearly grips to help pull the inserts out.

"Remove them," Lanar said over the com, "but don't bother welding them shut again. We'll come back around to reinstall them after we've lived another day. I want comm silence except to tell us when you've cleared an insert."

Wes unhooked his welding tool from his suit and held it up, activating it. The blue light of the laser reflected off his helmet, obscuring his expression.

Tadeo's muscles tensed as Wes ran the laser along the rectangle, each movement painstakingly slow, until the edges of the insert turned a bright orange. He tugged at the grip. Almost immediately, orange faded to dull black, the metal cooling, and Wes lifted the power cell insert up and out, while Tadeo held his breath. He activated his helio and leaned in to look at it. It looked just like the new one had in Dritan's cubic—glowing yellow strips coated the entire metal rectangle.

"Insert number one. Clear," Lanar said.

"Insert thirty-four clear," Wes said. He slid it back into place, and they moved two steps to the right to work on the next one.

"Insert sixty-seven clear," Cind said.

Sweat dripped down Tadeo's forehead, and the salty sting of it ran into his eyes, but he couldn't wipe them. Wes started the process again on the next insert, and Tadeo's stomach twisted with each careful movement of the laser.

"Insert sixty-eight clear."

"Insert two clear."

Lanar and Cind reported, their words on top of each other.

Wes pulled out the next cell, and Tadeo held his breath again. Yellow strips. No explosives.

"Insert thirty-five. Clear," Wes said as he slid the insert back into place.

Wes began running the laser along thirty-six and pulled it out. Yellow strips. "Insert thirty-six. Clear."

More reports flooded in. No bomb. That

was at least nine now of one hundred. All clear.

Tadeo stepped up to thirty-seven behind Wes, heart pumping, his mind clear. The adrenaline surging through his veins made him feel more alive than he'd felt in long time. He was doing something for the fleet. Something worthwhile.

But maybe he was wrong about all of this. Maybe the explosives were somewhere else. Command level. The galley. Medlevel. Regardless, the president and board would be off the ship until he and the guard could remove the threat.

The comm crackled, and a loud voice came through. "Lieutenant Raines. It's Kiva."

"Report," Tadeo said.

"The command level families are loaded up in the transport. Chief says he'll be heading our way soon with more squads. He'll be here in thirty minutes."

"Good. Thank you, Sergeant. I need comm silence until they arrive."

"Yes, sir."

Wes completed the next insert. Clear. They were all clear. Had Tadeo truly been wrong about the threat? About everything?

Wes started on the next insert, carefully heating up all four edges.

"Cycle coming through in a few seconds," Lanar said into the comm. "Stop what you're doing."

Wes kept going with the laser, not heeding Lanar's words.

"He said stop," Tadeo warned.

Vibrations coursed through the corewalk, and everything shook. Tadeo gripped the handrail, struggling to hold on as the core shuddered beside them, and the flimsy metal platform moved beneath his feet.

Wes's laser shifted and sliced across the rectangle. *Through the insert.*

Tadeo's pulse quickened to a dull roar in his ears.

Wes deactivated the welding tool, and it clattered to the platform as the shaking ceased. Tadeo kept one hand on the handrail and reached out with the other gloved hand to grab Wes's sleeve.

"What the fuck did you do?"

Wes turned to meet his gaze, and Tadeo saw his eyes, no longer obscured by the glint of his laser. They looked wild, terrified beneath the plasstex.

Tadeo's blood went cold, and he lunged for the insert. Wes blocked him and shoved him backward.

"What's happening?" Lanar's voice.

Wes shoved Tadeo again, harder, and Tadeo fell back on the corewalk. He grabbed the railing and pulled himself upright, his every sense on full alert, even as the corewalk swung, unstable, beneath them.

Wes stood a foot away, gloved hands balled into fists, his eyes crazed.

"What are you doing?" Tadeo said. "Move out of the way!"

Wes lunged for Tadeo, but Tadeo stumbled back just far enough to avoid him.

"You killed Tati," Wes said, his voice shaking. "You should've been the one—"

Tadeo charged him, tackling him to the corewalk.

"What's going on?" More voices questioned on the comm, but Tadeo barely heard them as he and Wes wrestled on the swinging walk.

Wes angled his body low, and managed to wrap his arms around Tadeo's legs and haul him half over the railing. Tadeo lost his breath as he glimpsed the long fall to the bottom. He darted one arm out to grab at the rail as gravity and Wes tried to throw him to his death.

"They lie to us." Wes panted. "I loved her, and you—"

Tadeo punched Wes's helmet, and his head snapped back. But he only pushed against Tadeo harder, forcing him farther over the railing.

He was going to die.

Tadeo did the only thing he could, the only thing that might give him a shot at survival. He let go of the handrail. And he nearly toppled backward over the edge.

But with both arms free, he grappled with Wes, and by sheer force of will, managed to shove him sideways onto the corewalk.

Breathing hard, Tadeo sank back to the walk and wrapped his arms around an off-balance Wes. He heaved him high, forcing *him* over the rail this time.

As Wes went over the railing, he yelled, scrambling to grab hold of something. He grasped Tadeo's arm and managed to hang on.

Tadeo hesitated for a moment, straining against Wes's full weight, as the corewalk swung wildly.

Wes's eyes were wide, bright. "Soon

there'll be a new order."

"Not today." Tadeo pushed Wes away, forcing him to release his grasp, plunging him to his death.

As Wes fell, a scream erupted through the comm.

Tadeo blinked, dazed, as the scream reverberated in his ears, drowning out all other communication. Wes, in his white suit, tumbled down, past the corewalks. His body bounced off metal, and snapping sounds traveled through the comm. The screams grew anguished. Then a thud as his body hit the floor. The screaming stopped.

Silence on the line.

Only the sound of Tadeo's own blood pumping, his own rattling breath.

Only the hum of the power core vibrating through him.

Voices shouted, all trying to talk at once, and Tadeo whirled to face the power cell insert. He gripped the ring and pulled hard. The insert came free, and Tadeo's hands shook as he stared down at the interior.

No yellow strips.

A clear plasstex container was adhered to the insert. And within it—black powder flecked with white crystals.

He leaned closer, hoping what he saw was just a trick of the light, but he already knew what he was seeing was real. The plasstex had melted around the outer edge of the container where Wes had cut through the center of the insert.

The white Zenith crystals were glowing.

CHAPTER TWENTY-THREE

Tadeo gripped the insert, feeling too dizzy to stand, but he somehow managed to stay upright. The crystals were glowing. How many minutes did they have before it blew up?

The voices finally cut through his fog.

"What happened to Wes?" Lanar's voice, booming through the comm.

"He tried to throw me over the handrail. I threw him over instead," Tadeo said, not hearing his own voice.

Then another surge of adrenaline moved through him, knocking the dizziness away. He carefully walked back toward the ladder he'd come up, holding the insert out before him. "I've located the bomb. It's active. I repeat, the bomb has been activated. Get down to the platform and get the main doors open. Evacuate the sublevels now."

Tadeo's voice sounded calm, commanding, like it came from someone else.

Tadeo tuned out the chorus of panicked voices and focused only on the insert in his hands. He swallowed the metallic taste in his mouth. *One step at a time.*

He had to get this away from the power core. The further away he got it, the more people might survive. Where was the closest airlock? There was no time. Anywhere on this ship, hundreds or thousands of people would die. Including him.

Tadeo reached the ladder and started down it, his legs still shaking. He gripped the insert with one hand while lowering his body with the other.

"There'll be another cycle soon," Lanar said, his voice cracking.

The combined weight of Tadeo's suit and the insert made hanging on to the ladder difficult, but he held on with everything he had, slowly working his way back to the main platform.

When he reached the last rung, the

ladder began to vibrate. He stepped onto the platform and gripped the guardrail with one hand as the entire platform and scaffolding shook.

They were waiting for him on the platform, all of them, faces drawn. Omar stood beside the main doors as they creaked open.

Kiva ran in from the corridor. "I commed Chief," she said, breathless. "He's coming—but he's on zero deck."

Everything seemed to be moving in slow motion. His body felt heavy, like he was sinking in a vat of uncured soyad.

"No time," he said. "Are the president and board away?"

"Yes."

He looked down at the glowing Zenith crystals. Where should he take it? He had minutes. But how many? His gaze moved to the corridor beyond Kiva. If he sprinted, he might make it to the airlock at the other end of the core. The one where they'd airlocked Era.

Tadeo strode past everyone, the stuck feeling fading. "Kiva, Omar—clear the sublevels. Get everyone to safety. I'm sending this fucker out an airlock. Go!"

Tadeo ran down the corridor. How long did he have? Two minutes? Three? It had already been at least five minutes since Wes had hit the bomb with the laser. At least. Maybe longer.

The suit and the heavy insert made him slow, and he pushed against the extra weight, trying to move faster. But the harder he ran, the farther away the other end of the corridor seemed. His legs were shaking too hard, slowing him down. This thing was going to blow up in his hands.

It would kill a lot of people if it went off now. And it might destroy the Repository—end any hope of ever rebuilding civilization on a new Earth. Even if he didn't survive, the archives *had* to.

Tadeo blinked against the sting of sweat running into his eyes. He glanced down at the bomb, his breath catching painfully. Were the crystals glowing more brightly than before? Or was it a trick of the flickering lumes here?

He raised his eyes and stared down the corridor. *This isn't a bomb. I'm not in space gear. I'm just on a planet with real gravity.*

He tried to picture a new Earth, like he had so many times while running the levels on the *Meso*, like he'd imagined while running the treadmill on the *Paragon*.

A new world. Blue skies. Open fields. Green trees. Dirt paths. *Life*.

His legs strengthened beneath him, and he sprinted toward the end of the corridor. He was running fast now, his body under his control again, and the end grew closer, until he was there.

Breathing hard, his side stitching up, he fumbled for his shift card on the loop around his waist. He ripped it off, scanned it, and pushed into the control room before the door finished opening.

He ran to open the door that led to the airlock. It seemed to take forever to open, but once it did, he stumbled inside and laid the bomb gently on the metal floor of the airlock. Then he scanned his card to get back into the control cubic.

As the door slid closed behind him, he took two steps to the control panel and typed in the same code he'd typed in two nights before, when he'd airlocked Era. Red lights began to flash in the airlock. He could barely hear the sirens through his helmet, but he knew they'd started up on the other side.

The black powder mocked him from the other side of the airlock, and the crystals appeared to glow red beneath the lights.

The countdown had begun. *One minute.* Too long. How long had it been? How long did he have? Tadeo backed away from the glasstex separating him from the bomb. Soon the airlock would open, and the bomb would be swept into space. But would it be soon enough?

He couldn't leave without seeing it go, and even if he did leave now—if it went off, he'd be dead anyway, and it would probably take off the entire side of the ship. At least the Repository was on the opposite end. The *Paragon* might be crippled, and thousands would die, but the dekas could salvage the archives and keep going. And not under new leadership like the terrorists wanted—like *Wes* had wanted. The board and president were safely away.

Tadeo kept his eyes glued to the countdown. Thirty seconds. The bomb had to be seconds from exploding. He should be terrified right now, but he only felt high. High on danger—exactly how he'd felt all those times he'd snuck down to the sublevels on the *Meso*. All those times he met Kit in secret.

PARAGON

Kit's laugh. Her green eyes. The way she'd sounded when they'd moved together, two hungry bodies in the dark. In unused stairwells, in helio sector during night shift, in sublevel storage, in places they never should have been.

She would have gotten her implant in a month. But he'd convinced her to break the rules, and she'd paid the ultimate price.

It only took a few times before he'd gotten her pregnant. Tadeo's eyes burned beneath closed lids. His mother had tried to protect them—had kept people from finding out the child was his. But Kit refused to talk to him after the day she found out.

It was an illegal pregnancy—set to be terminated whether it was defective or not. In truth, it was treason. He and Kit had committed treason when they'd had sex before she'd gotten her implant. They'd disobeyed the population laws.

And the day before Kit been scheduled to abort, she airlocked herself. Just like Era.

Except *he'd* airlocked Era.

Tadeo opened his eyes and looked down at the teardrop tattoo on his wrist, one-half of an infinity symbol.

Quin crops failed from rot if the right balance of nutrients wasn't maintained. Maybe the universe had a balance, too. And maybe he was on the wrong side of it. Maybe this was his sacrifice. Maybe this was the way he needed to atone for all he'd done wrong.

Tadeo looked back at the countdown.

00:10

00:09

00:08

The outer door would be opening now.

00:07

00:06

00:05

00:04

Tadeo wiped the sweat from his brow, and the tightness in his chest let up.

00:03

00:02

00:01

00:00

The inner door cracked open, revealing space beyond, and the bomb was sucked out.

His muscles relaxed, and the heaviness lifted, leaving him giddy. He'd done it. He'd saved the ship.

Bright light exploded around him, and all sound died. A force slammed him backward into something hard and unyielding. It knocked the air from his lungs, and he felt his bones snapping.

Had Kit thought of him before she died?

He gave in and let the darkness carry him away.

CHAPTER TWENTY-FOUR

Dritan woke, feverish, in the darkness. Burning pain tore through his arm and radiated down his body, crippling him. Sweat soaked his clothes, his brow, and he reached out blindly atop the rock pile, seeking his helio.

His hand found the familiar cool sphere, and he tapped it. It floated beside him, illuminating his progress. He'd cleared an enormous pile of stone, but there was still no sign of a door, or the corridor that should lie beyond here.

The painmod was gone, he'd drunk the last of the water hours ago, and McGill still lived, but kept going in and out of consciousness. Dritan was on his own.

He checked the line on his oxygen pack. *Red.*

The helio started to bob and weave unevenly through the air. It was about to die. And so was he.

Dritan snatched the sphere from the air and turned it off, gasping as another surge of pain ripped through him. He lay on the rocks, panting in the pitch-black. Hazy memories drifted through his mind, brief fragments, moments in time.

His mother, smelling of lavender soap. Era's scent. Where had his mother—a sublevel worker—gotten exec standard soap?

When he was small, he heard a story and went to ask his mother about it. She held him in her lap, cuddling him close. "Do you know what 'A Better World Awaits' means?" she asked him.

"No, Mama."

"Well, see, that scary story you heard wasn't the whole truth. Our ancestors *did* destroy our home planet. Some people say the old gods of Earth cursed us to roam space until we could be forgiven. And if we all do our part—work to ensure the fleet survives—one day we'll be redeemed—and then we'll find our better world. And so we say 'A Better World Awaits.'"

"What are gods?"

Mama's eyes widened playfully, and she kissed his forehead. "Beings. Like us, only more powerful. But, buddy... that story was wrong. The old gods *didn't* curse us. And they didn't forget us, either. You're my proof. You're *blessed*."

"Blessed?"

"The gods made you lucky, Dritan."

He fought back the haze, fought against the memories or dreams, or whatever they were. Exhaustion threatened to overcome him, but sleep would only mean death. He couldn't give up. He had to fight till his last breath.

"Haven't I proven myself?" he said into darkness. The air felt thin, and he coughed. "Everything I've ever done has been for the good of the fleet—for the good of my family. What else do you want from me?"

Dritan reactivated the dying helio and hauled himself higher on the rocks, closer to the top—to try to clear more there—to try one last time to find the exit. It took every bit of strength he had to reach the top, and when he did, he collapsed again.

Then the ground shook. The damn planet was determined to end him.

He clutched the rocks around him, desperately trying not to fall, as the entire pile shifted. Pain screamed through him, razing up and down his arm, and tears ran down his cheeks in response.

Then it ended, leaving Dritan lower than where he'd been.

He ground his teeth and moved to the top once more. One hand after the other. Each time he gripped a rock with his bad arm, flashes of light danced across his vision.

When he reached the top of the rubble, he was shaking, and sweat poured down his brow. He reached for a rock with his good arm and pried at it, willing it to move. And when it did, his helio glinted off... something.

Dritan's heart thudded faster. There, at the top edge. *Metal.* He'd been near here earlier, but it had looked like layers of rock between him and the corridor. But the quake had shifted things. If that was the corridor...

His breath came in shaky gulps, and new hope sprung up within him. He dug into a rock and pried at it. It didn't budge. He gripped it with both hands, and with a guttural scream, tore the rock away and let it fall to the ground below.

Black crowded his vision, and he nearly passed out. He reached up and touched the spot where he'd seen the gleam, running his hand along it. He choked back a sob and remembered the shape and feel of every scar and burn he'd gotten in the metalworks on his home deka.

Home. He'd recognize the surface he touched anywhere. His hand ran along the edge of a panel, rivets under his fingertips—metal forged on the *London*.

He pulled at another rock with all his might, gasping from the pain. It rolled toward him and bounced down the rubble to the ground. Metal glinted back at him, dusty, dinged, full of promise. He worked faster, pulling at the smallest rocks, trying to gain purchase to move larger ones.

Each breath he took grew thinner, the oxygen pack nearly gone. After a few fevered minutes, Dritan reached in and found *nothing*. He lifted his body higher, trying to see. A deep hole of blackness stared back at him. He had to risk testing the air beyond.

He lifted his mask and pressed his face to the gap to take a tentative, small breath. If it was Soren air, his lungs would burn with the plasma of a thousand cores. But they didn't. Instead, stale air flooded his nostrils. He took another breath and another. Blackness didn't close in, dizziness didn't overcome him. The air was sweet, if dusty.

The corridor beyond this wall still held oxygen. He tore off his mask, throwing it away from him with the empty oxygen pack, and poked his head and arm through the hole at the top of the doorway. He threw his helio down into the shaft. It illuminated more rock below and the dusty panels of the corridor.

Excitement flooded him, and he inched forward, twisting as he went, squeezing through the hole he'd made to the other side. But his arm gave out, refusing to work, and he lost his grip.

He rolled down the pile of rocks, each one like a bolt of steel going through him, until he hit the bottom. A horrible, heavy coldness smashed into his skull, and a new warmth dripped down his brow. His helio winked out, leaving him again in pitch-black.

He took shallow breaths and tasted

the salty metallic tang of blood as it dripped down his cheek and found his lips.

His lungs ached, and the agony of his mangled arm flooded his mind with pain and nothing else, making it hard to think. Had he been wrong about the fresh air in here? Did he get this far just to die anyway?

The haze washed over him, more memories flitting past. He was hallucinating.

The warmth of Era's lips on his.

Gentle pressure on his good hand, squeezing three times.

I. Love. You.

Tears gathered in Dritan's eyes as the deep thrum of the power core rumbled through him. He was dying. There was an accident in the sublevels. But he'd sacrificed himself for the good of the fleet.

A bright light came to take him into death. Soren's sun—gone supernova. His eyes fluttered shut, but the light only grew stronger.

Voices.

Dritan forced his eyes open as a globe of light resolved into a helio above him.

A masked, blue-suited woman crouched beside Dritan and held a new oxygen mask to his mouth. "It's okay. You're safe now."

She turned around and shouted back up the shaft. "We found a survivor!"

DEFECT
PREQUEL TO THE
LEGACY CODE SERIES

Selene Hayes is a genetic experiment gone wrong.

Damaged.
Broken.
Defective.

World hunger has been vanquished, but drug-resistant diseases kill millions. The corporation that gave Selene superimmunity called her Protected... until they discovered the truth.

Now they hunt her and those like her, and Selene's been hiding off-grid for eight years to avoid capture.

But she can't hide forever. Rumors of a new threat—and a mysterious quarantine—have reached her sanctuary. And if Selene has to fight, she'll fight until she dies. The Corporate Coalition will never take her alive.

LEGACY CODE SOUNDTRACK

Autumn Kalquist and music producer Freya Wolfe have created an official soundtrack for the Legacy Code series.

Please visit **AutumnKalquist.com** to find out how you can listen to "Better World", the song featured in this book.

"BETTER WORLD" LYRICS

Wanna stay here with my dreams
Don't wanna face the day
'Cause this reality's my nightmare
since you went away

Everywhere I see your face
In every song I hear your voice
Like a phantom melody
Why'd you make that choice?

I wanna believe I'll see you again
I wanna believe that this isn't the end

Wanna believe that there's a better world,
A better world awaiting
Better world waiting
Waiting
Waiting

Wish I could find faith in what they call lies
Since the day we lost it all, and the old gods died

And everywhere I see your face
In every song I hear your voice
Never got the chance to say good-bye
Before you made that choice.

I wanna believe I'll see you again.
I wanna believe that this isn't the end.
Wanna believe that there's a better world,
A better world awaiting
Better world waiting
Waiting
Waiting

Need hope the dead religions give me
Want a reason, not a chaos theory

Wanna believe
I'll see you again
Wanna believe
That this isn't the end
Wanna believe that there's a better world.
A better world waiting
Waiting
Waiting

FRACTURED ERA SERIES

DEFECT

DEFECT: PART ONE
DEFECT: PART TWO
DEFECT: PART THREE
DEFECT: PART FOUR

LEGACY CODE

LEGACY CODE
PARAGON

ACKNOWLEDGMENTS

Thanks to my dad, mom, stepdad, and sister, as well as all my family and friends, for your love and support. It means a lot to me that you're right here with me, wanting to see the fleet get to its destination!

To Erynn Newman and Bethany Kaczmarek, I love working with you both! I'm so lucky to have such wonderful editors.

Thanks to Jamie Blair and Freya Wolfe, for the many hours you spent helping me make this book what it is.

A special thanks to my beta readers: Alicia Porter, Emmanuelle Pensa, and Sita Payne Romero.

And, of course, I couldn't have written this book without the unwavering love and support of my husband and daughter. I love you both, and you help keep me grounded lest I lose myself in my worlds.

CPSIA information can be obtained at www.ICGtesting.com
Printed in the USA
LVOW11s1801090216

474361LV00007B/840/P